PRAISE FOR
THE SMILING SCHOOL FOR CALVINISTS

'Duncan has a tender, moving, poetic voice that lingers long after the laughter . . . original, inventive, ambitious, playful, funny and a million miles away from the current stereotype of the laddish Bloke's First Book'

Independent

'With knockabout humour, implausible plots and even less reliable narrators, Duncan recalls Mark Twain . . . a hugely entertaining read'

The Times

'It would be hard not to like *The Smiling School for Calvinists*: inventive, well-crafted and ripe with affection for its characters and settings, this is a beautiful debut from an imaginative and intelligent writer'

Scotsman

'The poet Don Paterson is right in comparing Duncan to Borges . . . one of Duncan's key ingredients is a tender fascination with the recklessness of childhood'

Guardian

'I laughed and hooted, wet-eyed. No really, I did . . . which is not to say that all the stories are amusing. Many are tender, reflective. Some are tragic. All are moving . . . the satire is at the same time gentle and wicked, affectionate and hostile. Duncan is an excellent writer'

Derek Beaven, author of *If the Invader Comes*

'Duncan draws on the surreal folk-baroque of pub-talk, anecdote and urban myth . . . insert some point about the schizophrenia of the Scottish here or maybe it's best to let Duncan and Boat Rab speak for themselves'

Time Out

'Fasinatin' . . . here comes anither yin, ye cry. And well you might; anither scary looking baldy fella frae the east o' Scotland bangin' on aboot the peculiarities and idiosyncrasies o' his toon and its folk . . . but Duncan diz the incredible; he makes ye want tae actually go tae Broughty Ferry . . . he kin convey the maist simple o' tales wi' untold energy and vigur, and a plaintive brilliance that wid make the sternest o' fowk's lip tremmel'

List

The Smiling School for Calvinists

The Smiling School for Calvinists

Bill Duncan

BLOOMSBURY

First published in Great Britain 2001
This paperback edition published 2001

Some of the fiction in this volume has appeared in the following publications or been broadcast on radio as follows: *Chapman:* 'Baather wi a Snake' and parts of 'The Smell o the Sea'; *New Writing Scotland:* 'Bather wi Weemin'; *Shorts: The Macallan/Scotland on Sunday Short Story Collection*: 'Boys, Girls, Games'; *Northwords*: 'On Leaving a Volume of Soren Kierkegaard's *Fear and Trembling* in the Back Room of the Campbeltown Bar, Dundee'; *Without Day: Proposals for a New Scottish Parliament* (Pocketbooks 2000): 'Tenebris Petimus'; BBC Radio 3: 'The Thatched Roof, the Roadside Madonna and the Banjo'.

Bloomsbury Publishing Plc, 38 Soho Square, London W1D 3HB

A CIP catalogue record for this book
is available from the British Library

ISBN 0 7475 5757 8

10 9 8 7 6 5 4 3 2 1

Typeset by Hewer Text Ltd, Edinburgh
Printed by Clays Ltd, St Ives plc

Thanks to
Sam Boyce, Rosemary Davidson,
John Glenday, Jim Petrie

Thanks to
my mother and father,
Scott, Niall, Grant,
Fiona

Dedicated to the memory of
Iain Crichton Smith (1928–1998)
Francis Boyle Surgeon Wilson (1912–1981)

'In one Broughty Ferry hostelry I was pleased to make the acquaintance of a venerable seaman of advanced years, who had joined the crew of a kelp harvester as a boy of nine. Decades of exposure to sea and weather had created upon his left temple a ridge of small but perfectly-formed barnacles. This singular decoration he displayed with a quiet pride and nursed in an affectionate and proprietary fashion with regular dousings of Tay seawater . . .'

from *Northern Jaunts*
Dr Alexander Jamieson, 1856

'To the east of Dundee nestles the fishing village, its face turned away from its near-neighbour, as if jealously guarding centuries of habits and customs. The history of the village can be heard in the wind, smelt in the sea-spray and witnessed in the austere faces of the men and women who still go about their business in the harbour and nearby streets: Puffin Wynd, Boat Lane or Seal Close.

A two-mile journey westwards, and it is difficult for the modern visitor to find signs of the city's maritime past. The whale-processing factory is now a nightclub, the warm glow of the whale-oil lamp replaced by the glare of neon and the flash of stroboscope; the chant of the flensing song has long given way to the thump of techno and the strutting brag of gangsta rap. The curing shed, where once the skins of Polar Bear, Arctic Fox and Walrus were stretched and dried in their precious thousands, is now a DIY Megastore.

Only the endless clamour of the gulls among the tenements and multi-storeys, pulls the visitor's gaze towards the sea, changing from green to grey to silver, linking village to city; past to present . . .'

from *Scotland: a Guide for the Independent Traveller*
Robert McBride, 2000

Contents

Dundee 1½
Broughty
Ferry 3½
Maritime
Heritage
Trail

Extracts from the Catalogue of the North-East Maritime Heritage Trust Collection

88. Hand Harpoon
Double-barbed. The earliest known example in Scotland, made in Dundee in the eighteenth century. The small reversed barbs or 'stop-withers' were added mid-nineteenth century. These were designed to catch the network of fibres within the blubber of the whale, preventing it from pulling free. The harpoon is inscribed 'SS *Aurora*' on one side and on the other 'Boab fae Dundee'.
Total length: 110 cm

92. Flensing Implement
This item has a curious hook-shaped head and a socket for fitting a shaft. Its exact use is unknown but it may have been employed in the flensing process.
Found in car park of multi-storey in Blackness area of Dundee, July 1998.
Total length: 40 cm

95. Blacksmith's Die
Used to sharpen the barbs of harpoons.
Dimensions: 13 × 9 cm
See item 88.

104. Umbrella
Made aboard a Dundee whaler. The handle and rib ends are of walrus ivory, the ribs of whalebone and the hood of sealskin.
Length: 79 cm

120. Plate from a Child's Book
Illustrating an Arctic scene, captioned

'The Manner of Killing Bears on the Coast of Greenland'. The plate has been hand-coloured.
Dimensions: 25 × 18 cm

129. Child's Toy Seal
Made aboard a Dundee whaler. Life-size, made from the entire skin of a seal pup, stuffed with jute. Harpoon mark visible on left side.
Length: 50 cm

145. Working Model of a Walrus Grab
The device was used to hoist the walrus aboard the deck by hooking into its tail flippers. Designed and patented by Thomas Bruce of Clepington Road, who sailed with the SS *Narwhal* to oversee the first operation of the grab, which came to be widely used aboard Dundee whalers.

151. Keel-Hauling Apparatus
Reputed to have been used during the early days of the Dundee whaling trade, aboard the SS *Hardship*. Consisting of rope, leather harness, hardwood and brass winding gear. Probably manufactured at the yard of William Courage and Sons.

174. Scrimshaw Work
Tooth of a sperm whale. One side engraved with the figure of an Eskimo, the other depicting the whaler SS *Baleena* in pack ice with a large ice-berg in the background. In the foreground two men flense a walrus. Inscribed 'To my beloved Elizabeth'.
Height: 16.5 cm

179. Scrimshaw Work

Eardrum of a blue whale, perforated with five fingerholes and mouthpiece. A type of flute commonly used to accompany dancing and shanties. Engraved with a scene depicting the whaler *Eskimo* sailing past the Tay Bridge on its return to Dundee in 1894.

Dimensions: 18 cm × 12 cm

192. Tin of Preserved Whalemeat

Bearing the label 'Robert Stephen and Son, Arctic Wynd, Dundee, 1846'.

Height: 19 cm

The Smell o the Sea

1

The trail begins outside the Flenser's Arms. Face the sea. Walk to the end of Harpoon Street, cross the road and pass the old seal-flaying shed. Directly between the visitor and the sea stands the figure of a large fisherman, broad shoulders hunched as if in protest against the prevailing south-westerly. His right hand shields his seaward gaze, his left arm supported by the shaft of the large flat-bottomed bait shovel he leans on. The visitor will be struck by the man's stillness and his apparent indifference to everything but the sea, which on some days laps playfully close to his feet, on other days drenches the oblivious fisherman in a whirling maelstrom of spray. Still the observer is likely to be perplexed, noticing the heavily barnacled wellingtons, the intricate lattice-work of his string vest, the detail of the interwoven fibres of the stout rope supporting his trousers. At this point the visitor will become aware of the simple bronze plaque at the base of the meticulously rendered wooden monument:

BOAT RAB – FISHERMAN (1906–1999)
Carved, painted and varnished by his beloved friends
'FEAR A BHATA'

One of Rab's friends accompanied me to the statue under a grey north-east sky, his commentary providing a fitting epitaph:

That's Boat Rab. Ane o the aald-style Ferry folk. A Fishin Man. No a Dundee Man. Ninety-three years in the Ferry an never been tae Dundee once. Said there wiz nothin in that toon but 'thieves, hoors, comic singers, sand-dancers an mince-worshippers'. Ye'd easy recognise Rab – no the smartest lookin lad in the Ferry but presentable enough. Big RAF grey duffel coat on in aa weathers, string semmit clean on every day, pair o black bus-driver's breeks held up wi an aald bit boat rope an a pair u wellies wi the taps turned ower. Hud ane ur twa funny habits, mind. Hair wiz aye immaculate but it wiz aa din wi mulk. Ehh. Mulk. Rab's hair wiz sleek as an eel's back an black as the Earl o Hell's ridin baits, gleamin like a shillin oan a darkie's erse. Rab widnae yaize Brylcreem or onything – up in the moarnin, a guid skelp o mulk on the hair, combed right back. Looked fine tae, but see in the summer in the waarm weather? Jesis. It aye went sooer, sometimes rancid an a couple o times it turned intae butter on Rab's heid. Hell o a man tae stand next tae in a pub in the summer.

Ehh. That's right. Wee cottage in Long Lane. Some hoose. Rab wid be doon the beach at low tide first thing, diggin up the lugs fur bait. He'd bring them back wi the bloodworms an plunk the hail lot doon in a giant-size Ostermilk tin in the middle o the livin-room table. The wife got a hell o a fleg when she stole a look in the tin ane day an the hail thing wiz slowly movin wi worms o various colours an sehzes. Swore she'd never set fit in thon hoose again. Never did. Some ither funny habits tae, him an Jeannie. Rab didnae believe in cookers an rarely yaized a plate. Naw. Ehv seen me sittin in Rab's hoose an there's Rab wi a great big flat-bottomed bait shovel, cookin the tea ower the fire. Ehh, in the shovel. A skelp o butter an a couple o handfuls o wulks an Rab's bent in front o the fire wi the wulks clakkin aboot an sizzlin wi Rab whustlin 'Stranger on the Shore' in that mad shaky whustle o his wi Jeannie an the Admiral lookin on. That's right. His doag. A Hebridean seal-huntin hound. Biggest doag in the Ferry. Rab yaized tae tie it tae the leg o the livin-room table wi ten feet o tow rope. Wan day the Admiral caught the scent o a seal on a south-westerly an that wiz him. A breenge through the livin-room windae; smashed gless, rope, table, lugworm fleein aa ower the place, the lot. Through Jeannie's washin, draggin table, bedsheets, claesropes, long johns, bloomers an Jeannie efter him. Rab took bad wi the wey the Admiral ended up, though. Latterly, the baist hud some condition whaur its private bits started tae inflate tae the stage whaur there wiz mair ootside the doag than there wiz in it. Ehh. Correct. Rab buried it oot at sea wi full naval honours. Flung it ower the side at Mad Man's Bank. Rab swore he would never tak up wi anither doag efter the Admiral, but fur a time he did go aboot wi a burd. Naw. A great black-backed gull. Trained it up fae when it wiz a chick an waandered aboot wi it perched on the shither o his duffel coat. The burd went lame in wan leg an Rab fitted it up wi a widden ane made fae a spar o timber. Some say the spar wiz aff a carriage salvaged fae the Tay Bridge disaster. Big vicious bugger o a thing, though. Attacked a couple o pensioners in Woolies wan Setterday moarnin an no lang efter that it turned on Rab in the Eagle bar. Rab wiz munchin intae a packet o scampi fries an the next thing he kens the thing near taks the hand aff him. Wid it tak no fur an answer? Mayhem in the pub – Rab's tryin tae protect his heid at the same time as grabbin a haud o the thing, which by this time's screechin, flappin an dive-bombin a faimly o holiday-makers eatin their haddock an chips. Well, Rab got haud o the thing, stuffed it intae his duffel coat an wrung its neck ootside the Tourist Information Office.

Aw definitely. A Great Man fur the fishin. The fowk in Long Lane were never withoot fish when Rab wiz on the go. 'How are ye aff fur fish?' he'd say, then him an his three muckers wid be aff wi the boat he kept in the loabbie. Boat Rab, Wullie the Puffin, the Maist Ignorant Man in the World an the Submarine Commander wi an upturned rowin boat on their heids, away through the middle o the toon; past the Indian restaurant, ower the zebra crossin, past the electrical shop an intae the Tay. How did they ken whut wey tae go wi a boat on their heids? The smell o the sea, son. THE SMELL O THE SEA.

2

A short bus journey rewards the visitor with stunning seascapes and from the upper deck of the Number 37, the coastline of Scandinavia is visible on a fine day. The visitor should alight directly outside the museum.

A paddle, a mit, a boot: all that remain in Dundee Museum to remind visitors of the extraordinary story of the Eskimo who arrived in Dundee under bizarre circumstances and made our city his home for two short years. The story of Chikanuk, the Sinderins Eskimo, is recalled by Euphemia Gibson, 103-year-old daughter of Edward, one of the men who discovered Chikanuk that winter morning in 1903.

(Euphemia told her story to the author, who transcribed it into Standard English.)

A cold December day in the Baltic Dock, and my father and his two mates were unloading horse carcasses on to the whaler Narwhal. Taking a break from this strenuous work, something caught the eye of one of the men, and the three went to investigate. They were astounded to discover the form of an Eskimo, slumped semi-conscious in his kayak.

The fellows assisted the man into a dockside hostelry and, presently revived by the hearty company and flowing spirits, Chikanuk held the circle of dockers in thrall with his tale, communicated to the men by my father's mate, a fluent Inuit-speaking cabinet-maker from Lochee. Caught on a stray current during an Arctic storm, Chikanuk was carried far from that dazzling but inhospitable realm, through nights of groaning bergs and gnashing floes, through blinding aurorae and howling blizzards, to awake into a fine Dundee morning.

There being no whaling ship voyaging to the Eskimo's homelands until the departure of the Baleena the following spring, Chikanuk took up lodgings with a harpooner in Tait's Lane. Chic soon became something of a celebrity in the West End, where the folk were not slow to take the appealing fellow to their hearts. He quickly became an attraction in the crowded Hawkhill taverns, regaling the appreciative companies with his store of Eskimo legends and folk songs. His rendition of 'The Walrus and the Maiden', yodelled in Inuit and broken Dundonian, was a particular favourite which delighted the ears of many. To see Chikanuk in the Empress Ballroom on a Saturday night, waltzing in full Arctic regalia, was indeed an unforgettable experience.

Being of an exceptionally cheerful and gregarious disposition, Chikanuk became involved in a wide range of community affairs, an especial highlight being his visits to local primary schools. What finer visual aid could be presented to children studying the Arctic than a live Eskimo in the classroom? Ever eager to entertain and delight, Chic would share with the children his beloved repertoire of Arctic lore. Bessie recalls, as a youngster at Hawkhill Primary, Chikanuk playing a nose-flute of his own invention, ingeniously fashioned from the tusk of a walrus. His performance of 'The Boy, the Girl and the Igloo', complete with dance and mime, delighted the young charges in Miss Simpson's primary 7. Some of the more immoderate of Chic's illustrative actions, however, left Miss Simpson (who declined Chikanuk's spirited invocations to participate) shaking and ashen-faced.

A particular favourite among Chikanuk's young audience at Blackness Primary was 'A Boy and his Beluga', an Inuit whale-flensing song, delivered with stupendous gusto, while four of his young charges acted out mysterious rituals under an old blanket, representing the skin of the leviathan. The same children were no less delighted when, on arrival in the playground one January morning after an unexpected snowfall, they discovered an enormous, expertly built igloo. Such was the degree of skill exercised in the edifice's construction that it served for some days as a makeshift classroom when burst pipes rendered the primary 6 classroom inoperative.

With the passing of the seasons and with Chic's apparently happy adoption of Dundee, some folk began to see the Eskimo as a permanent feature of Dundee's West End. Alas, with the onset of a second winter, Chikanuk's heart was pining for his frozen homelands. One morning he gazed wistfully at the slowly falling snowflakes drifting around the life-size walrus he had built in the back courts for the amusement of the bairns. The next morning he was gone, leaving nothing but a paddle, a mit, a boot, a host of happy memories and a pair of scrimshaw penguins which, to this day, have pride of place on my mantelpiece.

3

Returning to the Flenser's Arms, examination of the lime-washed harling to the right of the entrance will reveal a row of rusted iron rings bolted into the wall, the only set of boy-tethering rings remaining in the north-east. The evenly spaced indentations to their right mark the positions of a further three. As many as eighteen boys at a time would be tethered to the rings while their fathers slaked their thirst within the hostelry.

The practice was, apparently, less cruel than some commentators have suggested. The length of rope employed was sufficient to enable makeshift recreational activities to occur and games of football, dancing or boxing bouts were commonplace and occasionally simultaneous. The boys would, in later years, tether their own sons to the rings, upholding a tradition not uncommon among the menfolk of the fishing communities of the north-east.

A copy of a faded postcard can still be purchased from the museum, depicting a line of fourteen tethered boys smiling broadly under the caption:

Greetings from Broughty Ferry,
Seaside Holiday Capital of the North-East

4

Cross the road. Approach the sea, keeping the statue of Boat Rab to your left. Turn right and walk fifty yards. The observant visitor arriving at low tide will notice Mad Man's Bank, the treacherous low-lying sandbank, which has its part to play in the following account, narrated by another of Boat Rab's friends. Enter the public bar of the Ferryman's Rest.

That's the skin o ane ower there.

Tae the left o the gless display case o the eel swallyin the ither eel.

Ehh. A big square o it, nailed tae the waa. Looks kindo like an aald bit grey tarpaulin the now. That's cause it's been caald the last few days. A good spell o sun an it slowly grows shiny an golden, smooth tae touch, like a cross between velvet an fur. When it's stormy it goes aa damp wi wee silvery-grey metallic scales. Best o the lot is when it's been snowin a few days an it starts by turnin slightly prickly then grows intae a mass o tiny pure white feathers.

Never needed a barometer in this pub. Ye can yaise it tae tell the time o day too.

Ehh. Some o the regulars can tell the day o the week fae it an also the mood o the wife. Ahab says it's aa tae dae wi the phases o the moon, the pull o the tides, the ambient sea temperature at Broughty Ferry an the degree o charged particles in the upper atmosphere. Aa this affects the grain o the skin an the leh o the fur.

A strange baist, mind.

The maist difficult animal in the world tae tame.

Never turn yer back on ane.

Tak the hand aff ye soon as look at ye.

Only knows one master an aye liable tae turn roond an kill him.

Kills fur the sake o killin.

See Ahab? Ehh. Lad ower there wi the World War Two flyin helmet, black goggles, leg missin an one airm. Lost the airm in a tangle wi ane o them on a sandbank on the Tay in the middle o the night when he wiz a young man. Tore his erm clean aff, scuttled intae the watter wi it an awaa. Ahab swears he heard laughin. Never saw that erm again. Bones waashed up at Carnoustie next day, though. Picked clean.

Ehh. Ahab vowed tae get revenge an became a bounty hunter. Wiznae lang before he lost a leg in a fight wi ane in the foothills o the Sidlaws. Last he saw, it wiz flappin ower Auchterhouse Hill wi his leg in its claas. Claimed it wiz the same ane he fought wi on the sandbank. Swears they never forget a man's face. What else wid ane be daein sae far inland? Ye'll have heard they come on land at night, hidin up trees, skulkin aroond outhouses or even stealin a night's sleep in a bed.

Ehh. Stories aboot them interferin wi weemin or even stealin a bairn well documented. Worst of aa is when ane gets aald an its pincers, claas an fangs wear doon an it turns man-eater. Usually content wi the odd porpoise or seal. Gorges itsel then rests up, lyin low fur a few days in a sea cave or an aald hulk o a boat. Never sleeps an has never been seen wi baith eyes open at the same time. Occasionally gies fermers baather at the lambin season when they'll tak a few tae feed tae their ain young. Mind you, aa this never stopped some lads in Dundee fae tryin tae keep them as pets.

Ehh. Disnae mak a good pet, though. The grandfaither kept ane in a Lochee tenement for a couple o months an it wiz fine at the start – good wi the bairns an that. Things soon went wrang, though, an ane day it flew through the windae wi his wife efter stranglin the Alsatian. His brither yaised tae tak a young ane oot fur a walk on the end o a lead but ane day it juist turned roond an killed him.

Rarely survived captivity.

Naw. The owners.

Correct. Aye the man they'd kill. Funny that.

Naw. Naebiddy ever tried breedin them, but the Submarine Commander did find a clutch o eggs laid in a seal trapped in his nets an brocht them hame an put them by the fire at night. On the stroke o midnight they hatched oot an ran up the chimney an ower the rooftaps.

Ehh. Wee perfectly formed anes, aboot six inches high, complete in every detail includin the lang shiny curved spur on the back o the leg. Efter they escaped they smelt the sea an by the time they got tae Boat Lane were tirin a bit, half hoppin an half flutterin, makin that strange trillin squeek the young huv, halfwey between a moose an a blackburd. Anywey, Ahab wiz comin up fae the beach wi his big flat-bottomed bait-diggin spade so that wiz the last o their bid fur the sea.

Flung the carcasses tae the monkey when he got hame.

Ahab's done a lot o readin up aboot them an he says they appear in stories an pictures way back. St Columba wrote aboot seein ane aff Iona and an Irish monk did a fancy drawin in the Book o Kells showin one o them stranglin a sea serpent. Ahab has a tattoo based on it on his back. Hae a look at some of the Pictish stanes in this area an ye'll see a huge brute o an unidentified baist killin things.

Ehh. A few. They've officially been hunted tae extinction, but there's a couple still spotted aff the coast o Barra an there's a huge white ane seen beh fishermen roond the Shetlands. The fishermen keep quiet aboot this, mind. They're happy wi them because o the number o seals they tak. Whenever a seal gets caught in a net, which as often as no is because it's tryin tae chew through it tae get at the fish, the men'll either club it tae death or shoot it through the heid an keep it fur the next sightin, or maybe leave it in a remote bay whaur they'll find a skull an mebbe a flipper a day or so later.

Naw. Personally eh widnae like tae see them makin a comeback.

Naw. A lang time since ane wiz seen aroond here. Fifty years ago Ahab harpooned the last ane aff Mad Man's Bank.

Ehh. That's its skin.

Lookin stormy. Accordin tae thae feathers a wind backin

south-south-west, gale force over exposed easterly coastal areas wi a ninety per cent chance o thunder on Tuesday an a severe depression passin ower the wife.

No thanks. I'll be gettin hame but Ahab'll tak a double.

5

The last feature of the Maritime Trail takes the visitor past the Ferryman's Rest to the remains of the small pier adjacent to the eel-smoking huts. An indistinct path begins amongst the net-drying posts opposite, leading up the hillside. The path rises steeply, affording impressive coastal vistas, until an airy viewpoint is reached, marked by the Dragon Stane, a fine example of a class I pre-Christian Pictish stone. The rectangular sandstone slab is impressive in its stark simplicity. On the side facing the visitor arriving from the seaward direction, the stone is incised with a fish-tailed serpent swallowing a man, whose forlorn legs can be seen protruding from the jaws of the monster. Approaching the beast, harpoon aloft, is a powerfully rendered bearded hunter. On the reverse of the stone the hunter is depicted plunging his weapon into the girth of the monster, which has now disgorged its hapless victim, whose exhausted form lies beneath the vanquished beast.

The stone is one of only three known to display the stages of a narrative on different faces. Despite the scouring effects of centuries of salt-laden winds, the stone, with its ancient story of maritime risk and triumph and the austere majesty of its setting amidst sea, clifftop and sky, provides a fitting conclusion to our trail.

The author acknowledges the generous support of the North-East Maritime Heritage Trust in the creation of this guide.

Grateful thanks to Wullie the Puffin, Euphemia Gibson and the Maist Ignorant Man in the World for their contributions. The forthcoming Internet version of the guide will feature their online readings.

www.com/the smell o the sea

A Bedtime Story

See thae jeckits? The big puffy silver anes like yer big brither wears? Ehh. The ane that maks him look like a cross between the First Man on the Moon an the Michelin Man? Well, when eh wiz a laddie in the Ferry eh hud ane like that. Except it wiz a special jeckit. A very special jeckit. Ye know how thae jeckits like yer brither's are made up o different sections, wi stitchin in between, so's the sections puff up braa an firm between the stitches? Mine wiz kindo like that, but we didnae hae the sort o fillin they stuff the modern jeckets up wi. Naw. Meh jeckit wiz fuhl o air. Ehh. Air. Ye hud tae blaah the jeckit up. It started as a shrivelled-up lump o wrinkled plastic, but when ye examined the garment closely ye discovered that each section had its own wee tab that ye pulled out tae reveal a clear plastic valve. Ehh. That's right. Juist like the wee valve on each section o yer paddlin pool, son. Except that it wiz yer jeckit that wiz covered in valves – aboot twelve o them. So ye'd open each valve up carefully between yer thumb an forefinger, blaah the section fuhl o breath an try tae replace the tab intae the wee airtube before any air escaped, so's tae keep each section nice an hard. Mind you, the catch wiz ye'd need so much air that beh the time ye'd managed tae get a sleeve inflated ye'd be blue in the face, gaspin fur breath an maybe even hallucinatin, as happened once or twice wi me. So as ye can imagine, an entire jeckit could take mebbee a hail efternoon tae inflate on yer own. However, if ye had a good team o pals like me, ye'd get them tae help. Wan laddie wid blaw up each section an it wid be a fine sight – a dizzen laddies puffin an blawin at a lump o plastic magically formin intae a jeckit, which ye would ceremonially put on when it wiz half-inflated. It's amazin whut ye could achieve through teamwork an cooperation. Later on, the same laddies frantically heavin an pechin wi bicycle pumps would speed up the process an cut down on effort.

Eh wiz the first in the Ferry wi the jeckit. Efter that, aa the ithers got ane tae. Eventually, though, the gimmick wore aff an folk started tae abuse their jeckits, sometimes over-inflatin them till they burst. Ye'd get ten laddies walkin down the road wi their jeckits aa hard an bouncy, makin big squeakin sounds wi the rubbin o the plastic. Occasionally, ye'd get a noise like a great sigh when somebody battered in too hard tae a harled waa an the jeckit burst. Sometimes two of ye wid charge at ane anither wearin over-inflated anes, an ye'd collide wi a thump an bounce back aboot six feet. One time, Boab, him they call the Creator nowadays, got a shot o the footpump his auld man yaized fur inflatin the tyres o his articulated lorry. Efter Boab accidentally burst six jeckits he got the hang o the thing and wiz able tae use it tae blaw up tae juist under burstin point, so the jeckit wiz incredibly hard an near spherical. Boab wiz stood there surrounded wi this thing like an inflated straitjeckit an he suggested that we should see what would happen if each o us could puncture a section at the same instant. When each o us, at the count o three, stuck a pin intae a section o the jeckit, there wiz a great hiss o air. Boab shot suddenly backwards an his feet lifted a few inches aff the ground. Boab wiz slightly shaken an a bit pale, but the rest o us werenae impressed. Afterwards, Boab juist stood there thinkin, eyes narrowed, lookin at Tam, the weest one o us, but no sayin anything. The next day Boab turned up wi a cylinder o helium, complete wi hose an nozzle, that his big brither got for him out the British Oxygen yard where he worked. Now Tam wiznae very happy about what Boab suggested, but he wiz wee an light and that's what Boab required for the experiment. Besides, Tam bein the youngest, he didnae understand about helium. Helium? That's what they fill the balloons wi at the carnival, like the wan you let go last summer. Aye – the big silver wan that shot straight intae the air, over the rooftops an away over the river tae Fife. Boab had once tried an experiment involvin his cat, which he let go of efter he hud tied six helium balloons tae it. I can remember his wee brither greetin as his cat floated out the garden, intae the street, across the road an away out o sight. Well, it took a lot o reassurin Tam that July day doon the beach, but once we convinced him that we would be holdin on tae a ten-feet rope he wiz a bit happier. We really meant tae hold on tae the rope, but, ach, we were laddies the same age as you an curiosity got the better o us. What happened? I wiz busy workin the valve o the helium cylinder, inflatin Tam's jeckit which wiz growin bigger an nearin burstin point. At this stage Boab decided it would be wise tae grab Tam's legs, an I could see he wiz strugglin tae keep him doon. Anither laddie saw this an grabbed the length o rope that hud been tied roond Tam's feet. Boab suddenly let go an Tam started tae float slowly upwards an quickly the rope went tight. Next thing the laddie holdin the rope started tae leave the ground tae, an half a dozen o us made a breenge fur him, grabbin on tae his feet. I dinnae suppose anybody meant any harm, but efter Boab whispered 'Let go!' Tam floated up over the beach, gently driftin over the sea, an I'll say this for him – there wiznae as much as a peep oot the laddie. But we started tae panic when we thought o what we would say tae his granny who wiz lookin efter him durin the school holidays. While we were makin our minds up Tam wiz floatin further over the Tay, then across tae the North Sea, an ended up in Scandinavia . . . Naw! I'm exaggeratin. That's no true. What really happened was that Archie, him that ended up livin wi the Eskimo, kept a cool heid and alerted the Broughty Ferry Lifeboat crew. They put the boat out, sent up a flare, puncturin Tam's jeckit wi the first shot. Tam dropped oot the sky like a shot bird an for a while efter some o the laddies called him Icarus Broon. By the time he wiz picked up in the dinghy, he wiz floatin in the still half-inflated jeckit. Later on, Tam became a great sailor, attainin the rank o Submarine Commander. Ye can still see the jeckit in Broughty Castle Museum, wi the big ragged hole made in it by the flare, wi the melted plastic aw aroond it. The press cuttins an photos are there too. I'll take ye tae see it on Setterday, if ye like.

Aye. Kind o like yer big brither's jecket.

Night, son.

Boys, Girls, Games

That's how the game started. Dark winter nights, nowhere tae go among the vertical streets but stand in the wind tunnel between the multis. We'd lean intae the wind, three of us: me, Pete an John, held up by the howl o the gale ragin through the narrow corridor o concrete. The idea was tae wait til it really screamed and lean with yer head as far in front o yer feet as possible an stay like that for as long as you could. A couple o times we managed tae stand like wrecked, broken puppets in the eye o the wind for ages. Once, when the three o us were suspended like that, I fought through the wind an stood in front o the other two, who didnae know I was there. I stood there leanin backwards intae the force, starin at them leanin forward. It must have looked like some weird urban ballet, wi the piercin white spotlights o the multis, an the three o us frozen in absolute stillness while the night howled about us. That one time I leaned back, starin at them wi their eyes closed, long hair whippin in front o their young faces, tranced and ecstatic. I knew then they would never be as beautiful again and that we'd never be as happy.

Once or twice the wind dropped in the middle o the ballet

an that wiz wild. A sudden wind drop an an ye'd be fightin for yer balance, maybe takin a lurch forward an swoonin towards the pavement wi a great uncontrolled heave. Once, Pete wiz standin there, tranced right in, freezin hands jammed intae the pockets o his Wrangler jeckit. By the time he realised the wind had dropped, he wiz hurtlin face first towards the concrete. Another night there were some crosswinds an eddies flyin around in the tunnel an I'm leanin sideways, totally still, screamin. It wiz pure joy when the wind wiz so mad ye could howl like wolves or roar or bark, just dependin, an the wind wid drown ye out. This one time I'm in the trance, the wind vanishes an I hurtle sideways an batter ma head off the harlin. The side o yer head crunchin wi the sudden shock o jabby stones, rakin yer hand through yer long hair an there's big spots o blood growin on yer white Wrangler.

To the right o the tunnel, the vestibule wi the nameplates we would gaze at: twenty-two floors, eight tenants per landing. One hundred an seventy-six spaces for nameplates; about a third of them permanent, another third changin every few months and the final third, the most interestin, permanently empty, but denotin flats occupied for years by people who didnae want you to know they lived there. Leftwards, the cellars. My key would open about one in three so sometimes you would be able to steal a bike or a cardboard box full of Christmas tree decorations and you could smash up all the coloured globes and fairy bulbs and set fire tae the tinsel on a summer evening. Best of all, though, we found a bottle o shellac and Pete knew what you could do wi it. He poured a trail o it round the concrete floor o the cellars, outside an back in again. One match fae the top pocket o his Wrangler an a big whoosh o flame hit the roof.

John wiz gifted too. That time he went out on a verandah on the twenty-second floor and hurtled down a Superball as hard as he could. A wee thing made out o dense, vulcanised rubber – reminded me o the material at the heart o a neutron star. We watched fae the playpark as it hit the ground and zoomed straight back up higher than the multi, disappearin from sight. The most unpopular girl fae second year wiz standin posin between two older lads over at the swings as Pete and I gazed up in the sky. Ye could just make out the wee speck gettin bigger an bigger an we totally froze in excitement when we saw it fifty feet above her head, hardly daring tae hope, but sure enough, the thing plummeted down, peltin right intae the centre o the crown o the stunned girl, hurtlin back up wi the momentum it gained fae the strike. The lassie just slumped stupidly between her two admirers while we swooned wi the joy o just havin witnessed perfection. In fact, the ball still had that much energy in it that it bounced half the height o the multi when it next struck the ground.

Around this time girls seemed tae be there more often an this led tae slightly better behaviour. Before all the excitement and confusion lassies were on the edge of our lives but soon they were occupyin a central role, clearin up some mysteries, but more often increasin them. A few years before this, girls were objects that intrigued and perplexed. Though ye couldnae quite see what all the fuss was about, sometimes yer pal's mother would be smellin nice an dressed up wi maybe a tight black jersey on at the new year an she'd give ye a big hug an a kiss an ye would feel kind o shivery an glowy at the same time wi strange stirrins ye didnae quite understand. Other times Pete would steal a *Club International* or *Escort* fae the top o his old man's wardrobe an the secrets o woman would be partially revealed in the form o the awesome, poutin, sullen creatures simultaneously evokin fear an desire. Before that I had been mystified after lookin at the reproduction sections in John's mum's medical encyclopaedias. I had been troubled at the cross-sections an drawins o female reproductive organs, complete with labels, Latin terms an arrows. I tried tae memorise the information in case I ever had the misfortune tae have tae use it. But it wiz hard tae visualise, an even harder tae relate these sombre medieval-lookin engravins wi the girls we were about tae know.

That wiz just the first o women bein puzzlin an difficult tae understand an things have stayed that way ever since, right enough. Ye didnae consider that girls were probably as fascinated as you wi all the stuff about sex, but I remember bein shocked when I got off the school bus an walked down the road behind the two best-lookin girls in second year; quiet, slow-movin, self-contained creatures. When we reached their street there wiz a couple o doags copulatin on the pavement. This led to averted eyes an embarrassed increases in walkin pace fae everybody goin past except the two girls who stopped an studied the spectacle wi cool, purposeful fascination, exchangin quiet comments an circlin the two animals, which by now were thrustin faster an faster, tae appreciate fully what wiz goin on fae different angles, inclinin their heads tae obtain a variety o viewpoints.

Pete, who wiz the most fascinated by dirty stuff, would bring in the instructions fae his mother's Tampax an we huddled together readin an thinkin o all this applyin, no just to our mothers, but to Sheila an Irena an Helen, who were fast turnin intae mysteries. Pete wiz always fascinated by devices like that an it wasnae long before he was bringin in packets o condoms an showin ye them an makin ye look at the instructions even if ye werenae that interested, which ye probably were. Mind you, once or twice Pete's incredible ignorance o the things he wiz fascinated by gave us a laugh. Like the time when we were on our way tae a party which some girls we fancied from our class were goin to. Pete sidled conspiratorially up tae me, produced a packet o Durex Gossamer an enquired as to whether I was puttin mine on before I went or if I wiz just waitin til I got there. Later, he admitted tae never havin used one in earnest, but spoiled it all by tryin tae salvage his credibility, claimin that he had masturbated while wearin one an that it worked. Pete wiz the first person who ever brought in real filthy pictures, which his big brother had acquired when in Denmark on a school cruise. Once, he produced a photograph o a man, fat wi hair like Elvis, wi his penis in a woman's mouth. I wiz confused. I couldnae see the point o doin a thing like that; it just seemed stupid. The man looked fed up an still had his socks on, an the woman looked a bit like my auntie. All the fascination wi condoms didnae help Pete anyway – he married at seventeen tae a girl he got pregnant. The last I saw o Pete wiz a couple o years ago. He wiz in a scheme pub playin for the darts team. He wiz fat an wearin a Rangers strip that said Gazza an I looked at him an he looked at me but nobody spoke.

It wiz John discovered the coffin recess. We didnae know at first that the black space behind the two doors at the bottom o the brushed silver aluminium o the lift interior wiz for putting bodies in. Well, no bodies, but coffins, but it made sense when somebody explained it to us. All five o the multis had one, of course, but the faraway one, for some reason, wiz never locked so that's where we went. At first it wiz just for the daftness o bein in there; you an yer two mates, stuffed intae the dark, box within a box, glidin up an down as people called the lift from all floors throughout the multi. You had tae be really quiet, obviously, so the folk in the lift wouldn't know ye were sittin there, a couple o feet away fae them. You could look out at them too, if you sat beside the keyhole, but you really only saw from their waist down tae their knees, unless it wiz a bairn, dependin on where they were standin. One night, this man came in wi a woman an John wiz at the keyhole an told what they were doin on the way up tae floor twenty. I'm no sure if I believed him, but after that there wiz always a lot o shovin an arguin about who wiz sittin where, until we resolved the situation by organisin a proper rota for coffin-recess positions. Nobody ever saw anything as excitin as that ever again, though. I only saw a drunk pissin an Pete says he saw the insurance man masturbatin.

Normally the coffin recess was more what ye would describe as an aural, rather than a visual experience. There was a lot tae listen to, right enough. Most folk never said aa that much an most o the time they were in wi other people they only ever saw in the lift, so it'd be pretty routine stuff; good mornins, an caulder the day an stuff like that. Sometimes a bit different, though. A couple o drunks once started arguin about the time o high tide at Wormit an this led tae violent verbal abuse followed by actual blows which continued tae echo down the corridor away into the distance as the lift descended. The commonest rows were between husbands and wives comin home after the pub – merriage is a joke an the joke's on me, if you smile wance mair at that bastard eh'll thump baith yer pusses an so on.

More interestin was how people spent their times when they were on their own, or thought they were. A lift's a strange kind o space; public but seeminly private. Once the door shuts it's a bit like bein in the bathroom, though certain folk took that idea a bit far sometimes. Few people would remain silent; most would hum, sing, whistle or talk tae themselves aboot all manner o things. Once or twice I heard somebody quietly greetin an felt a bit rotten. Usually when folk on their own talked it wiz funnier, though, mutterin on about shower o bastards, or, her sittin there wi a puss like a burst settee, or whatever. The best times were when the lift went really quiet an just the click o the windin gear, the slide an thump o the doors an the glide o the cables. The passenger in the lift would maybe whistle a couple o bars o 'Magic Moments' an John would say somethin under his breath but no quite. He would talk in a slightly quivery, strangled voice on the edge o panic an say somethin like please, no more, or Jemima or simply heave a low moan or maybe clear his throat briskly an businesslike. He usually managed tae get it just right. Of course, ye couldnae see their reactions, but things would usually go dead quiet for a few seconds then the person would cough loudly and the hummers would hum louder an the whistlers would whistle no tune at all slightly more hysterically. Sometimes folk whose breeks ye recognised would get off at the fourth floor instead o the twenty-second, where they lived and the lift would go up empty.

The game stopped when Pete had a rush o blood tae the

head an opened the door when somebody wiz still in the lift. The woman looked down in horror as the doors slowly opened, followin a series o low moans between floors, tae see three fourteen-year-old boys squashed intae the coffin recess. There was nothin for it but tae bolt out an make a dash past her as soon as we could stop at a floor. Next day, the coffin recess wiz locked an that wiz it.

After that, there wiz years o patchouli, dope, girlfriends, drugs an women but these were the best things; the wind tunnel, the ballet an the coffin recess. The last time I heard o John he wiz in the local paper: 'Kirriemuir Man Brandishes Hammer at Wife'. I didnae realise he had moved, or got married. Seeminly he felt bad about bein described as a 'Kirriemuir Man'. I heard he had a leg off soon afterwards then died. Pete had his name in the papers for wife-batterin no long ago an more recently faced charges for the sale an distribution of obscene materials. I'm still teachin.

Baather wi a Snake

The wife's mither hid an affy baather wi a snake last week. Ehh. She still bides doon the stairs fae us an she's daein no bad fur her age but eh thocht it wiz the end – screamin an roarin an baalin an furniture gettin shoved aboot an glesses smashin an things thumpin aff the waas. A hell o a cairry-on. Ehh. The wife's faither's no daein too bad either but it wiz partly him tae blame fur aa the baather. Him an his brither the Submarine Commander – him that breeds the ostriches in the back gairden – arranged tae dae some fishin doon near the herbour, no far fae the sewage outlet. Noo as ye'll know there's a hell o an eels doon there. No much ither fish because o the condition o the watter but the eels like it. There's some really big anes tae – seeminly they feed on the seagulls doon beh the sewage pipe an they'll also tak the occasional rat. Aw ehh. Eh didnae believe it either till eh saw it wi meh ain ehhs. A big ugly bugger o a herrin gull – ane o thae shitehawks wi the big glowerin puss an a pair o shithers like a Hilltoon bouncer – peckin aboot among aa the muck. Naw. Dinnae laugh. Yer talkin aboot a nutrient-rich environment there wi aa the barnacles, limpets an mussels breedin ower the rocks. No that yed eat them yerself of coorse, but yer man the burd's peckin awa, occasionally throwin anither gull a hard look when – ye'll no believe this – this thing wi a fais on it like somethin oot a nightmare coils oot the sea, opens its jaas, grabs the burd beh the feet an haals it under wi a flurry o screamin an flappin that flung aa the ither burds up in a big squawk. Noo you tell me whut thon bugger Attenborough's daein wanderin aboot wi walruses at the South Pole an monkeys in Amazonian rainforests when aa he needs is a camera crew doon beside the shitepipe at the Broughty Ferry sewage outflow. An if ye dinnae believe me look up any encyclopaedia an ye'll find that the eel is a right bastard that'll survive in any waater – the mair polluted the better. A mature male – the bull eel – will attain a length o six feet an feed on near aathing that moves includin crabs, fish, rats an, evidently, burds. Wance at the sea-fishin, the Submarine Commander netted a fehv-foot eel wi anither eel jammed twa feet doon its throat an the rest o it still stickin oot its mooth. Eh suppose the human equivalent wid be me trehin tae swally you. An aboot the rats. The Maist Ignorant Man in the World saw an eel catchin a rat an downin it in a wanner AND he claims it's no such an unusual event either. As ye know the eel will come on land an ane moarnin when Ignorance wiz diggin up lugworm he saw a couple o rats scuttlin aboot among some o the rubbish. Just at that, a ripple in the waater caught his eye an then this big bastard o an eel sneaked oot the low tide an slid tae where the pair o rats were busy fightin ower somethin daid they hud got a haud o. Cool as ye like yer man the eel's in among them wi a pair o jaas like a trap roond the rat which beh this time is twitchin an squeekin wi its squeals becomin fainter an fainter as its tail disappears doon the gullet o the eel which juist slides back intae the sea.

Anywey, that day the wife's faither an the Submarine Commander decided tae go fur the eels as they were havin nae luck wi anything else. It wiznae lang until the wife's faither hooked this great brute o a thing wi an eye that could juist aboot turn ye tae stone if it caught ye lookin at it. Soon enough the Submarine Commander belted it a guid thump aboot the heid though it fairly danced an jerked aroond fur a couple o minutes efterwards. Lookin at the thing it wiz aboot fehv feet lang – an aald bull eel wi its sides aa scartit fae fightin. The Submarine Commander suggested the wife's aald man get it stuffed an mounted in the pub beside his ain display o the eel swallyin the ither eel in the gless case. Ehh. The wife's faither drinks there regular. That's whaar they went efter the fishin wi the eel stuffed in a Tesco bag. The twa o them got on the blether an what happened next wiz the wife's faither walked oot the pub, went hame an fell asleep in the chair waatchin the TV. Forgot aboot the eel aathigither. The Submarine Commander noticed the Tesco bag wiz still lyin there, but decided there wiz nae hurry an efter anither couple o Rum an Green Gingers he waandered doon tae the wife's faither's hoose wi the bag. Beh this time the wife's faither's fast asleep an the wife's mither, wha's goin a bit deef, is makin a start on the hoosework. So the Submarine Commander rings the bell a couple o times an when naebody replies, he decides juist tae leave the bag ootside the door in the closie. Noo juist before he went oot intae the street he decides, mebbe fur safety's sake, tae go back up the stairs an stuff the bag through the letter box. The wife's mither wiz daein her usual; listenin tae a musical on the radio, singin alang wi it an gettin on wi the dustin. When she gets oot tae the loabbie she spots the Tesco bag an thinks that's kindo funny but then she notices the bag twitchin a wee bit. Kin ye imagine the wife's mither's horror when she sees the bag startin tae move aboot the flair wi the eel's heid pokin oot it, lookin aa aboot? Correct. No deid. Stunned. Eh, STUNNED, an still alehv. Next thing the eel's oot the bag, twistin aboot the flair an the wife's mither's howlin an screamin aboot snakes an the wife's faither's awake an the twa students fae up the stairs burst in thinkin that mebbe thon scene oot *The Exorcist* is takin place doonstairs. As it happened ane o the lassies wiz a marine-biology student an while her pal calmed the wife's mither doon, she took the eel awa an put it in her bath till she wiz able tae cut it up fur her studies.

So the wife's faither's still in the bad books but, as he says, there's nae legislatin fur the Submarine Commander when there's an eel aboot.

Tenebris Petimus

Walk along a city-centre street. Observe the dour buildings, brooding under a glowering sky. Glance at a passer-by and witness the scowl thrown at the smiling stranger. Look to the rugged mass of the Salisbury Crags, setting for the Ettrick Shepherd's masterpiece of sin and depravity, looming like judging Elders above the emerging Scottish Parliament. Gaze beyond to the cold glimmer of the Forth as a mean smirr of rain drifts across the November dusk gathering over the city. Our heritage of darkness and cloud. Our people, happier in shadow and drizzle than in light and sun. Our Parliament, emerging below the ancient volcanic detritus of the crags, reaching into the millennium and millennia beyond.

My proposal spans our past and future, reaching into the primal bedrock of our psyche, while employing a twenty-first-century interface of micro-electronics, marine biology, psychiatry and ergonomics. I propose the development, manufacture and distribution, via our public-health authorities, of the Caledonian Darkness Box. This invention will aid the hundreds of thousands of Scots whose lives are blighted by the depredations of seasonal affective disorder during the spring and summer months, tolerating the untold annual hell of extended daylight hours and increased sunlight. The author can attest to the effects of summer depression: the nausea, the dawn sweats, the grinding afternoon headaches triggered by excessive light, the sudden and inescapable urge to flee to a sanctuary of darkness and cold. Panic attacks, sustained periods of convulsions and suicide are not uncommon in severe cases. The Box, secretly developed by a Broughty Ferry inventor, utilises fibre optics, high-performance outboard motor oil and a light-digesting enzyme derived from the secretions of the pineal gland of the giant Atlantic halibut.

Hitherto, curative therapy has proven either ineffectual or prohibitively expensive. One of the few documented cases of successful treatment featured a group of sufferers who spent the winter months in Shetland in order to maximise darkness absorption and the remainder of the year in Tierra del Fuego. This pattern promoted short-term emotional equilibrium but in the final analysis involved prohibitively expensive travel and subsistence costs. Various strategies initiated by self-help organisations involved groups of sufferers enjoying winter excursions to a custom-built timeshare complex within the Arctic circle, alternated with periods of summer residence on the Falkland Islands. Such initiatives, alas, proved only partially successful, and on return to Scotland, subjects drained their reserves of darkness before the end of summer. Subsequent remission periods involved dramatic mood swings combined with alcoholism and random violence.

The Darkness Box currently exists as a prototype in the form of a modified herring crate incorporating a front section which resembles a flat-screen television. The device is placed on any convenient surface and can be used indoors or outside. It is portable and ecologically efficient, powered by the natural light which is negated during operation. A series of points flicker then darken across the screen, coalescing into storm-like whorls which dim hypnotically, until the entire screen pulsates with negative light. Swirling masses of blackness sweep across the screen, creating a template upon which the subject can project the darkest of psychic imaginings, discerning within the Rorschach of abstract shapes a favoured rain-swept landscape, a glowering visage, a bleak urban wasteland or an absolute void. The inventor has created a series of relaxation tapes to accompany the device, and it is possible to stare into the darkness of the Box on a calm July afternoon while listening to the authentically evoked sounds of storm-driven hail lashing against rattling, ill-fitting window frames. A wide range of state-of-the-art peripherals includes the Dusk Simulator, an enhancement which ensures that the subject always awakes into a steadily darkening room on even the brightest June morning. The Ambient Chiller utilises a photosensitive thermostat which lowers room temperature in conjunction with the gathering darkness created by the Simulator. A screen-saver alternates the legends 'Tenebris Petimus', 'Seek the Darkness' and 'Speir the Mirk', rotating them silently against a background of complete blackness. For contemporary urban streetwear a discreet headset version incorporates earphones and goggles styled by John Calvin Klein. Currently in its final stages of testing, a Macintosh and PC-compatible software package provides a conversion kit which enables a home computer to be adapted for Darkness

Box use. It is, however, anticipated that the Spartan purity of the original herring-crate design is likely to appeal to those adherents with more austere tastes.

The contribution of the Darkness Box to our public and private lives will be limited only by our imagination. The benefits of widescreen boxes in public houses, restaurants, hospitals and pre-school playgroups will be obvious. Giant screens shall enrich civic life in cinemas, football stadia, public parks and city squares, promoting a sense of community and shared experience. For periods of quiet reflection or private contemplation, arcades and on-street booths should ensure that no one is ever far from a Darkness Box. These Boxes may be coin- or credit-card-operated, with a code allocated for free emergency use.

The inventor of the Box, a retired halibut flenser, is currently involved in advanced negotiations with an American multinational corporation who wish to install him as Director of Creativity for the Northern Hemisphere. It is possible that the level of remuneration, the research facilities and the lifestyle package may be enough to lure him to California from the research bureau, his wind-ravaged clapboard and corrugated-iron flensing hut. The first duty of our Parliament must be to ensure that financial support and research incentives encourage long-term residence of such innovative genius. Second, it must execute arrangements for the mass production and delivery of the Darkness Box to homes throughout the land so that every man, woman and child in Scotland enjoys unrestricted access to its benefits, regardless of wealth, creed or status. Politicians must take steps to ensure that the device occupies a central role in our culture and, to this end, can set no finer example than to arrange immediate installation in Holyrood, commencing every session of the Scottish Parliament with prolonged and solemn observance of the Giant Caledonian Darkness Box.

After Perfection

I'm sittin here an it's gettin dark already wi the news just on; shimmerin waves pulsin out the screen an crawlin across the walls as the room darkens wi the growin black outside an a voice tellin of disaster.

If I go to the reunion I'd see her. I want tae see her but I'm no sure I can bear it. The pain's there all the time but in the autumn it's worse an this year it's sorer than other years. The best season to be happy – spring or summer's too obvious – but the worst when yer low an remember too much. The way it seems tae bring the past back, makin ye think of all previous autumns, remindin ye of who you were then, what ye were doin, who you were seein, what they were wearin, what their touch felt like, their hair, the smell o her skin, her breath. No other time makes yer senses drunk in the same way. Try tae block it out, tell yerself it's just another phase o the year, the earth turnin on its axis followin its diurnal course, facin away fae the sun in an inexorable cosmic swing an the ache's still there. Only worse.

Leaves flickerin down fae black trees as soon as there's a wind an standin with yer eyes closed, listenin, an ye can hear each one o them landin in among the others. Bootin up big scufflin flurries in empty streets, the freshness o the cold an the smell an the touch of her, a low sun an the halo around her, baith yer breaths in the freezin air risin in one gleamin cloud. The past still comes unexpectedly alive – the drifting smell of burnin leaves, children's voices carrying in the dusk as it grows cold and dark, or a certain kind of music.

Rememberin means ye use fifteen-year-old malt tae help ye try an forget but it's no long before that helps tae make it worse again. The moist slidin pop as the cork squeaks out the neck, fillin a glass wi glintin amber promise, then ye end up rememberin more. It would be fine if ye could just erase the stuff in between an start there again. Rewind an press play an make everything different second time round. But reunion? Too much stuff happens makin everything different an I know I couldnae cope with the past bein so starkly there. No that I've anything against reunions, an it's no as if there was ever anything wrong wi the school or the people in it, but what can ye do when ye realise you've lost everything in a place between the past an now an ye cannae find the way back in?

It's hard tae imagine who o the ones I knew would go tae a school reunion anyway. We were mostly in the brainy classes o a senior secondary in the west end o the city, but still livin in housin schemes an workin-class homes an a bit wild really. Shopliftin quarter-bottles o whisky from the off-licence at dinner time an drinkin them in the boys' toilets an linin the drained bottles up neatly for the jannie tae find before goin to yer classes. Pete's mother worked in a chemist an told Pete that the pharmacist there had said tae her that Dimerol

Expectorant had a very high opium content an no tae take it when he had the cold and she would warn us against some other o the blacklisted medicines. So we would troop along wi our blazers on at lunchtime an buy a bottle or so each before the woman in the chemist caught on an stopped sellin us the stuff. It said on the outside o the bottle no to exceed the stated doze o 5 ml, but if ye managed tae keep down 125 ml o the viscous pink stuff without pukin ye could sit in history an point yer fingers at the walls an ceilins an bounce big flashin sparks off them. Pete once saw a lion when he wiz walkin past the garage on his way back tae school. Mandrax was more for the weekends: Pete's mum wiz on them because she couldnae sleep wi the strain o bringin up Pete so he would steal them an sell them in the corridor ootside oor Latin class. Taken with alcohol you would feel no pain as ye repeatedly dived head-first downstairs at parties in houses where folk's parents had gone out.

Just then the shopliftin became quite popular too but that only lasted a few months. We would take orders for Ben Shermans, Wrangler cords an Levi Sta-Prest, sellin them in the boys' cloakroom on a Monday mornin, if we had a good weekend. The craziest thing was the Hawaiian guitar which, once stolen, seemed useless, so we left it in a public toilet down the town. For a couple o days we remembered an laughed at the idea o somebody comin intae the smell o stale piss an carbolic on a dour mornin an bein confronted wi a shiny red mysterious instrument straight out o a Waikiki Beach Boys album. We knew the police had caught on to some of our activities an were pleased when the *Sunday Post* ran an article under the headline 'Cunning of the Modern Thieves Revealed' which described our technique for stealin LPs. In these days albums were often kept inside their covers in the shops an we invented a big square brown paper parcel wi a slit an a flap at one end that allowed ye to slide LPs by maybe Love, Clear Light or Spirit inside. Scary, though, was the reel-to-reel tape recorder; quality equipment an worth far more than we realised til Bruce, waitin for a late film tae come on, saw it described on *Grampian Police News*. A serial number wiz read out alongside a photograph o the item which we smashed up wi boulders the next day. That should have been the end o it but instead it came when Bruce wiz caught walkin out the door o the music shop wi a Hofner fiddle bass (the type used by Paul McCartney) inside his duffel coat.

Would Pete and Bruce go tae a school reunion?

So by this time I suppose ye were thinkin it wiz really time tae have a girlfriend an when ye finally started seein a girl, that wiz strange. From the first, I was always serious about girls, partly because o the music an how they were idealised in the songs I loved. It wiz an overwhelmin emotion if ye were like me; obsessive, extreme an desperate tae fall in love. At the time I would always be listenin tae painful, poignant music full o longin an loss an it wiz weird bein wi a girl ye loved instead of runnin about doin crazy things ye didnae really want tae do anyway. One night, Pete an I stole a bubble-gum machine from outside the newsagent's and fled from a police car then cracked the machine open wi a brick on the wasteland, leavin us a hundred threepenny bits, two hundred lucky charms an three hundred bits o primary-coloured bubble-gum balls an the pennies that hadnae already been emptied. Next night, ye would be inhabitin a world of emotions, idealisin yer girlfriend because ye were in love an had something secret an private like out o a book or a poem. Everything ye had thought about or heard about became real an it was the nearest thing tae perfection ye would experience on this earth.

Part of the trouble was maybe she could mean too much an the reality of her would never live up tae the the idea of her, especially when her image became intertwined wi the music that was the soundtrack of yer life. She wiz perfect an so wiz the music an somehow I could never cope wi beauty. Things that were flawless were unbearable an terrifyin when they were too close an you didnae really know what tae do wi them. All ye would end up doin was maybe violatin them or thinkin of destroyin them because deep inside you really felt you werenae worth bein near anything like that an it made ye dangerous an destructive. Some things were always better as ideas – best when distant an unattainable. Maybe I can never really touch beauty an can only harm it.

At least the music wiz genuinely unattainable: three-part American West Coast harmonies driven by janglin crystalline guitars, interlacin Baroque filigrees of sound, pure but strong. Words about love and perfection glimpsed for an instant then gone. It was somethin from another world – elusive an impossible. Gazin at the album covers, copyin them on to drawins for the wall, obsessed by the distant Californian coolness o the group wi their unsmilin, moody expressions, the letterin of the name on the sleeve romantic an medieval, heraldic, like a tapestry, gold an scarlet against the black, interwoven like somethin from the Book o Kells ye had seen in yer art class, an just soundin like perfection turned into sound though listenin to it made you uncomfortable an you knew there was somethin eerie an slightly uncanny about anything immaculate so in a way you wished it never existed. Maybe ye really thought about her that way too.

At the time it was floor six o the multi wi yer mum workin in the shop an yer dad gettin too old for workin shifts in the warehouse. You sharin a room wi yer big brother who wiz two years older than you an gettin intae Rangers an fightin an yer wee sister still sweet but gettin tough an swearin. The world you wanted tae live in wiz long straight blonde hair, fringed buckskin jackets, Californian shades, West Coast American accents; nothin grey, nothin housin-scheme, nothin Scottish. Nothin tae remind ye of yer real life. Everything tae help you escape.

Then I sensed another lad in the same year as me, who I had never paid attention to before, growin his hair longer an startin tae carry LPs about wi him; first American Blues an British R an B then American West Coast, an by the time we had been in the same art class for a couple o periods I discovered he wiz obsessed wi the same band as me. From the mornin he brought in their new LP the same day as it wiz released we were soulmates for ever. He wiz an only child an we were able tae spend most nights in his room listenin tae the music, learnin tae play guitars an wishin we could escape; yer parents, yer town, yer life, sometimes yerself.

The more ye got intae the music the more other bits o yer life became enemies; yer hair never allowed tae be long enough, yer way o talkin too Scottish, yer clothes never colourful enough an yerself never cool. The music became more an more an escape an ye wanted tae be part of it all. It wiz never the sound o summer, always autumn; the sound of somethin glimpsed, lost an pursued for ever. The sound o things that fade an die at the moment o their utmost perfection; like somethin touched an held for a moment before vanishin, worse for leaving a memory an a sense of loss always in yer life.

The same feelins found in the music gleamed for that short time in yer life with a girl. Everything glimpsed in the music became your own life's soundtrack an you felt it could never last an you were terrified when all the preciousness became yours but you knew your world couldnae deserve things like that. The music an yer life harmonised perfectly for an instant but really all the time it wiz happenin you sensed it slippin away.

Somehow you felt it wiznae right that you could have this much tae do wi beauty in the form of the slow-movin, perfumed, smilin creature wi her wee white dress an long black hair. She was to become part of your life briefly as the image of perfection an it wasnae fair that anybody should have to live up to so much an to be real an ideal at the same time. That's too much for anybody an that's how she was lost. There's been plenty other women since, some fine in their own ways an good women but every one sufferin from bein my attempt tae recreate somethin gone.

So, no reunion – she who ye lost could be sittin there relaxed an smilin, rebuildin the damage you caused her, radiant from the benefit o no sufferin from you any more. Or maybe even she couldnae bring you back the past an maybe she's no like that any more or never really existed the way I see her these years ago. Maybe that's the best way.

Never tae experience perfection because it spoils everything for ever.

A couple o nights ago I ended up walkin in the streets we used tae go to when we were together, at the same time o year we used to walk there. It wiz strange, like nothin had changed: same trees, same piles of leaves, same yellow lamp-post light wi the drizzle passin across it, like in a sad song. Only different thing wiz the occasional security light stabbin through the dark. An the years past an the changes in your life an things not there. Once I saw her in Tesco's. She wiz on her own an lookin nice an I knew that it would have helped if I had spoken tae her but I just left my messages, walked down the next aisle an out.

The leaves are whizzin past the window in a horizontal fury. There's a vast line o black cloud pressin down over the river, grey below an a thin band o silver gleamin bright in between an gettin narrower. The clouds are lowerin, driftin like smoke over the roofs. The trees are beginnin tae bend an the leaves are swirlin intae a blizzard. The windaes are rattlin an the silver line's disappearin as all grows dark an the first spots start tae lash off the glass.

The pane is covered wi great crashes o rain, splatterin an racin all over the windae, obscurin yer vision.

The reunion will be just startin.

Stanley's Inferno

The wife's side o the faimly still think o it as a howlin, smokin, sizzlin pit. Ither folk think o it mair as a state o mind. Maist folk dinnae think aboot anything at aa. The brither thinks he's been in Limbo this past quarter o a century waatchin 1–1 draws in the pissin rain surrounded beh the legions o the Damned gnashin an wailin in furious agony. Fat Stan claimed he experienced it twa Wednesdays ago at two thirty-fehv in the efternain when he fell through the trapdoor o the Gun, clattered doon the thirteen steps, blacked out fur fehv minutes, claimin he wiz deid an went tae Hell an back. Donald an eh witnessed the hail kerry-on.

Donald wid leave the trapdoor open when he wiz doon below changin the barrel or takin deliveries so the regulars, includin Fat Stan, were used tae it. A great dark door, aboot three inches thick, yawnin wide over the black hole o the cellar. Big gunmetal hinges an thick dull silvery-grey chains aa clankin when it wiz crashed doon like the draabridge o a castle fae medieval days. Beh the time eh realised whut wiz happenin Fat Stan wiz tumblin erse ower elbow doon the stairs. Him nineteen stanes, too.

When Donald an I got tae him, we jist exchanged a look, no sayin anything but fearin the worst. Both o us kent that leavin the trapdoor open wiz against all Health an Safety Regulations an both o us kent that the authorities would have the pub shut doon if they found oot that a drunk customer had plunged through a trapdoor that wiz regularly left open and gone hurtlin doon a rickety set o widden steps then thumped on tae the concrete flair below. Baith o us were wonderin whut tae do, kneelin ower Fat Stan, who seemed tae be flickerin in an out o consciousness. We were glad when he started mutterin, his head slowly movin fae side tae side, twitchin now an again. A couple o the regulars made their way doon the steps, one o them suddenly lurchin heid first an landin on Donald efter his foot caught in ane o the steps that Fat Stan had shattered on his wey doon. Archie reckoned it could be a bad move tae try tae shift Stan, but Donald wiz unconvinced an his mind wiz made up when Fat Stan started jabberin nonsense an shakin, movin his erms aboot as if wardin off blows fae unseen tormentors. 'Look! He seems tae be startin tae get back tae his old self again. Besides, he's survehved worse than this. Archie, you tak a leg. Tam, you tak the ither ane. Wullie an ehh'll tak an erm each . . .'

True enough, Stan had taken a few knocks in his time an this probably wiznae the worst. Some say he wiz never the same efter the hoose fell on him, though personally eh never saw any difference. He wiz a gaffer on the site whaar they were buildin the new sheltered-housin rehab centre fur Victims of Drug-Related Dangerous Dog Assaults an the project wiz yaizin the best o materials but a hell o a lot o the stuff wiz goin missin an turnin up in hooses aa ower the toon: baths, fireplaces, doors, sinks, kitchen units, the lot. Stan decided he wid stey overnight in the hoose keepin guard, so he put up the signs sayin 'DANGER – UNSAFE STRUCTURE. *DO NOT ENTER*' an settled doon wi his crossbow an a bottle o Navy Rum an the Celtic match live on the radio an the hoose fell on him in the middle o the night.

Fur a year or so efter that Fat Stan wiz on a wee bit o a downward spiral, hittin the drink hard an pickin up odd jobs here an there: teachin English in a secondary skail, mendin overhead power cables, workin wi a freelance rapid-response squad in the Lochee area. But we aye knew he wid mak a comeback an it wiznae long before he wiz there in his usual haunt, the Gun.

So the time Fat Stan fell intae the cellar, some said Donald wiz tae blame but Stan wiz a regular an knew all aboot the trapdoor. In fact, I wiz standin talkin tae him aboot who he fancied fur the *Stars In Their Eyes* semi-finals in the back room an looked up tae check the odds on the noticeboard – the Gulf War Veteran 5–4 favourite wi his Diana Ross turn – when Fat Stan, six feet two inches an nineteen stanes, vanished.

Ten minutes o heavin, pechin an roarin later, we got him tae the tap o the stairs an leaned him against the bar. When he came to, he started mutterin like he wiz in some kind o a trance an talkin in tongues – a great frenzied outburst makin nae apparent sense at first, though he gradually became mair lucid an it became evident that he wiz describin scenes fae Hell involvin the regulars oot the back room o the Gun. The strange thing about it wiz that Fat Stan wiznae talkin in his ain voice but once ye got over the initial shock o this ye could make out what he wiz sayin.

'Eh saw the Brain Surgeon bein biled an flayed alehv beh cacklin Dundee supporters. Wullie the Tortoise wiz bein branded wi red-hot irons sizzlin intae his flesh an smokin wi thick black reek. The Barkin Doagie wiz bein plunged in an oot o a vat filled wi seethin green acid, less o him comin oot each time. The Gulf War Veteran wiz swalleyed whole beh a giant craa, his feet stickin oot its beak afore he wiz vomited back oot then pecked up again. Eh saw the Weasel bein roasted, peeled, then runnin aboot, aa glossy. The North Sea Diver wiz bein stabbed beh a big smilin glamorous naked wummin wi lang shiny black hair an crimson nails like spikes that she stuck intae every part o his face an body. Eh saw me, hurtlin doon a dark tunnel, rollin aboot in agony in a black pit. Then eh ascended, lifted beh four shinin archangels taewards the light . . .'

The next day ehm standin chattin tae Donald aboot his plannin application tae build a boxin ring in the centre o the lounge bar when Fat Stan walks in, his face bruised an his erm in a sling, wi a crutch supportin the ither ane, but smilin, wi a look o unaccustomed calmness in his bloodshot eehs. Donald tilts a pint gless, puts his ither hand tae the pump, nods, an says wi a wee smile, 'The usual, Stan?' Fat Stan shakes his heid slowly, leans his crutch up against the bar, reaches intae his inside pocket an haals oot a roll o notes. He pulls the rubber band roond them aff wi his teeth, slaps seeven fifty-pound notes doon on the coonter an says, 'Donald – that's you an me aa squared up. Never sell drink tae me again.' Stan swivels roond on his crutch an hops oot, leavin Donald starin, slack-jawed, at the door swingin shut behind him, only movin when the beer overflows fae the gless ontae his shoes.

Fat Stan's no been seen since. Though the regulars sometimes think o him when they watch the blue light flashin an rotatin on the tap o the giant traffic cone wi the warnin siren that Donald aye puts oot now when he goes doon the stairs tae change a barrel. Some o the regulars went quiet the ither day, gazin at the whirlin blue light dancin aroond the walls o the pub, reflectin aff the bottles o the gantry an the solemn faces o those men that Fat Stan had seen in Hell twa Wednesdays ago, their talk silenced by the eerie howl o the siren in the half-empty pub.

JOB DESCRIPTION – HOUSING DEPARTMENT

Post Title: Senior Concierge
Section: Housing Management

PRINCIPAL WORKING CONTACTS

1. Chief Housing Officer for immediate supervision, allocation of duties etc.
2. Area Housing Office staff regarding any aspect of the service as it relates to buildings/environment and customers.

MAIN DUTIES

The postholder is required to carry out any or all of the following duties as they apply, either day or night:

1. Report immediately to the appropriate service all failures of lifts, pumps, engines and machines.
2. Liaise with police, fire and ambulance services to deal with incidents which may occur from time to time.
3. Supervise the ongoing programme of maintenance of rooftop space and helicopter landing pad, ensuring the area is secure and free of debris and obstacles.
4. Carry out weekly checks on the aircraft warning mast, checking structural soundness, ensuring that mooring bolts are securely fastened to roof and that all lights, sirens and alarm systems are fully operative.
5. Carry out regular checks on the roofspace of the tower, ensuring that no loitering takes place, liaising with appropriate external agencies regarding any potential or actual incident.
6. Ensure that lifts are utilised for the conveyance of tenants and their visitors between floors and that lift use is confined to this purpose: the use of lifts for illegal gatherings, entertainment or recreation is to be actively discouraged.
7. Monitor the use of coffin recesses in the lifts, in order to minimise abuse and promote safe practices.

8. Assist funeral directors in the execution of their duties in the event of death of tenants and/or their guests.
9. Patrol the building, including stairs, landing, lifts and roof to ensure that no unauthorised person or animal is on the premises.
10. On notification of exotic bird, insect or animal escape, assess situation, ascertain potential risk factor and, in partnership with appropriate outside agency, take necessary action.
11. Requisitioning of traps, cages, tranquillising chemicals, gloves and handling gear in connection with (10) above.
12. Ongoing maintenance of stun equipment in connection with (10 and 11) above.
13. General supervision of rubbish chutes and incinerators, with especial vigilance regarding use of the equipment for the disposal of animals.
14. Ensure that all communal landings are used solely as a thoroughfare between lifts or stairs and entrance hallways, and that the area is not used for the exercise of animals, for competitive games, or to provide additional cooking or sleeping quarters.
15. Discourage the use of balconies for purposes of barbecues, livestock breeding, distilling, karaoke, dancing etc. A comprehensive list of forbidden activities is not feasible, but in the first instance advice should be sought from the Area Housing Office.
16. Maintain a log of events in the prescribed manner.
17. Reduce or eliminate the noise, threat or danger caused to tenants by animals, children or other persons.
18. Report any use of flats for profit-making activities such as gambling involving animals or fowl, the production of motion pictures, or the holding of live performances.
19. Write incident reports as necessary, compiling and updating Incident Report file.
20. Undertake such other duties as may from time to time be deemed necessary by the Chief Housing Officer.

The Gravedigger

The Gravedigger took on a queer glower as the years passed, his face aa thon pale ghostly wey wi the constant blue-black six o'clock stubble shadowin the long, pointed chin. Never a beard, but never clean-shaven either. His claes aye dark an thon jet-black hair stickin straight up in big jaggy tufts. Personally, ehh never liked a man wi eyebrows meetin in the middle. Some said he minded them o a craa latterly.

The Gravedigger worked ootside fur the entire year. All summer he wid dig stripped tae the waist. Sometimes even in autumn or winter, tae. Strangest thing of all – he would never tak a tan. Diggin, scrapin, heavin, swallyin beer, twelve-hour shifts in days o heatwaves. Never swearin, never sayin anything, never lookin at anybody, never takin a tan. Efter sweatin in the sun fur weeks he wid still hae that pale, waxen skin, the colour o maggots or grubs. Never got dirty either. Queer that his breeks wid be streaked wi dirt an his boots clingin wi mud an the skin o his hands an face still pale.

Even in later years when he had long since stopped goin out tae the pub, he wid aywiz smell o alcohol. An him never without that taint o earth aboot him. His jaickit wiz black, right enough, but creepin ower it a greenish tinge, like an aald wall that never saw the sun. Near where he had been there would be a mushroomy odour clingin tae the air. His boots looked like they had once been black where ye could jist make out the leather beneath the soil that stuck tae them. They were more grey now an pale wi the mould that never seemed tae dry.

The Gravedigger wiz never seen without a rolly-up. The air always stained wi a smell o tobacco. Naebody ever saw him makin one an naebody ever saw him wi a new one but naebiddy ever saw him wi a dog-end either. Jist the same thinly rolled fag wi the half-inch o nicotine stain at the end. Some said it wiz the same fag all these years. The browny-yella colour matchin the finger an thumb o his left hand, the only part o him that wiznae grey, white or black apart fae the pale yellowish tinge o his eyes, aywiz bloodshot, the pupils aa black an beady, if ye managed tae look that lang.

Long efter he got out the lift o the multi he lived in, that stale reek o drink, sweat, cigarettes an earth wid remain. Once, a pal o mine went up tae floor thirty wi his doag – a black Labrador, normally a canny enough baist. Suddenly, ye could sense the animal startin tae grow restless, its shithers hunchin, its hackles risin an goin aa spiky, its eyes near stickin oot their sockets wi the whites startin tae show roond the edges, big yella fangs stickin oot fae quiverin purple gums as it slowly backed intae the corner o the lift, a low, menacin growl risin in its throat.

The last time anybiddy heard the Gravedigger speak wiz when the wife's Uncle Archie had been in the multi visitin her an recognised him as they came down in the lift. Seeminly the two o them had been great pals at the skail all these years ago. The wife's uncle wiz happily mentionin this when the Gravedigger looked at him wi that queer glower an said in a cold, flat voice, 'Don't know ye. Never heard o ye,' trundled his bike oot the lift wi his gravediggin tools aa clankin an cycled away intae the rain.

Seems the Gravedigger wiznae always like this, though.

The wife's uncle tells about when him an the Gravedigger were young. The Gravedigger's aald man wiz a gravedigger before him, allowin his son tae take his bike when he wiznae yaizin it himsel fur his work. Even then, the Gravedigger wid help his aald man tae dig the graves an sometimes when he had a shot o the bike he wid hurtle doon the Boys' ramp on that great big black message bike wi his aald man's gravediggin tools aa claarted wi mud, rattlin aboot in the big black tubular steel rack fixed on the front. The wife's Uncle Archie minds o gettin a lift an sittin in the rack wi the bike getherin speed an whizzin all the way doon the ramp, grindin tae a screechin halt at the bottom where Archie wid be shot out the rack an right intae the front door o the skail past terrified onlookers an the pair o them helpless wi laughter. Through time he wiz known only as the Gravedigger at the skail, most folk forgettin any ither name.

The Gravedigger wiz popular then, wi plenty o pals, many o them keen on the bikes. Archie an him wiz a great pair fur the cyclin an he minds o doin a three-week tour o the Highlands on a tandem that the Gravedigger had salvaged fae the dump, painted jet black an done up wi a fixed wheel an two pairs o toe clips. Archie said it wiz a hell o a pech up tae the Pass of the

Cattle but when ye took yer feet oot the toe clips an free-wheeled all the way down tae sea level wi yer knees bent an yer feet stuck oot tae the side it wiz like nothin on earth. By the time ye got back across tae the east coast ye had the hang o the bike an at the Berriesdale Braes they decided tae keep pedallin fae the summit, overtakin cars all the way down, takin their feet oot an the two o them jist aboot managin tae reach Helmsdale without pedallin, hurtlin crazily along for miles.

So it did seem queer the way he turned out in later years. As far as what went wrang, the wife's uncle says that the Grave-digger wiz never the same after he wiz helpin his aald man tae excavate a fresh grave up on the hill, where the cemetery wiz startin tae be overcrowded. It seems he disturbed an old grave he wiz workin in when he should have been at the skail, an Archie minds he kept talkin about it, horrified but fascinated in a strange way too an no able tae stop speakin of the pulpy mash o rotten wood, hair, soil, grubs an teeth. Archie thought maybe the Gravedigger wid give up on the work then, but no. From then he seemed tae grow more queer, no seein folk sae much an hardly goin out, apart fae his work. Ithers say he wiz strange from the start and werenae surprised at the way things developed. Maybe it was the line o work; maybe it wiz somethin else, something inside the man.

He grew more an more single-minded about work an finally obsessed by it. He left school early, takin over fae his dad when he retired an only wantin tae talk about his gravediggin. He wiznae much company an the few times when he did come out tae the pub, his conversation wiz all about graveyards, where new plots were bein dug, how burial wiz superior tae cremation, goin intae details about it that naebody really wanted tae hear. At work, most o the other gravediggers were deaf an dumb an he widnae learn sign language, an that suited him fine. Latterly, all the graveyards aroond here became full an he would seek work further afield. Ye'd see him leavin early in the mornin, lookin straight ahead, wheelin his bike out the lift. If ye spoke to him he widnae look, widnae blink, widnae say a word, just takin a wee skip over the saddle an pedallin away.

All this time him livin in the multi wi that nice wife o his, too.

Strange how life in the multi suited some folk fine but could break others. The both o them, her an him, came up fae the country when the Gravedigger's dad got him a job wi the city council. She never wanted tae leave the countryside, but it wiz said that in these days the Gravedigger had an easy way an a sweet tongue on him. Though she had the Carse in her blood she followed the man she loved, but never liked the city an never settled in the multi. She wid try to keep smilin as she always had, but something had gone. Makin the best of it, plantin out tubs an pots on the balcony wi honeysuckle, aquilegia, marigold an delphinium, an in summer she wid go out there an sit among her flowers, breathin in wi her eyes closed. Other times she would look west, where in wide skies above the Carse, the sun would go down over the river, a great blazin magnet drawin her heart. These times she would think o her family, an her an the Gravedigger never able tae have a child. One or two said the Gravedigger took bad wi this an went strange from then on. His wife never came tae terms wi her childlessness, her from the big family wi her brothers an sisters an their bairns. So there wiz her in the multi without the child she wanted an the Gravedigger growin cold an distant. For a while after movin into the multi she wid see plenty bairns; her family comin round often wi their families, so she wid enjoy the visits fae her wee nieces an nephews an their mothers an fathers. They wid like seein their auntie, comin up in the lift, lookin across the balcony tae where they lived, mixin wi the other bairns in the playpark, pilin on the swings, whirlin on the roundabout an comin back up in the lift, flushed an elated. Only, they stopped comin. The Gravedigger saw tae that. A word, a glower, the coldness; the sisters an the brothers felt awkward an the bairns unhappy an soon the visits became rarer an rarer. Once or twice she did allow the family tae take her back tae the Carse for visits, but that stopped too an after a while she began tae lose touch.

They were never seen thegether now, him only livin for his work, travellin further an further afield, doin overtime, Saturday an Sunday if possible, an sometimes overnight stays or longer, sleepin in remote huts an bothies in areas where few other gravediggers wid go nowadays. The more work he got the longer he stayed away an the more content he seemed tae be. Sometimes nobody would see him for days at a time an his wife wid only be seen goin tae the shops when necessary, her never socialisin, always preferrin tae stay in the flat. Even in the early days she never really liked pubs or clubs, but wid appear wi the Gravedigger, always pleasant an smilin but ill at ease among the lights an the music an the noise. It wiz a long time since the Gravedigger had been seen in the Gun, an nobody missed him, wi his long face an strange ways.

Folk started to wonder what life must be like for his wife,

livin on floor thirty wi thon cold, silent man, away from the house as much as he wiz in it nowadays. The two of them came tae be part of life in the multi; less an less noticed as time went by, people comin an goin, young couples movin in, havin bairns, movin away before the bairns were that much older. Never really noticed that much, just there; the quiet woman that folk felt sorry for an thon queer man that folk steered clear of. Many o the new folk that moved intae the multi as time passed never paid much attention; only a few noticed a couple of lives that seemed lost an sad.

If ye were tae read in a story about how it all ended ye wid hae difficulty believin it.

The Collector walked right intae the strangeness when he wiz daein his rounds in the multi. The lads afore him had given up efter bein set about once too often in the dark wind tunnels on winter nights by a gang o young folk wantin their money. The Collector wiz fine fur the job, though; ex-police, no long early-retired an supplementin his pension wi workin as a bouncer, daein private security work, money-lendin an a bit o debt recovery for the insurance company he collected fur. Great strappin lad, six feet two, broad shithers an a big ruddy face, greyin hair cut intae a crew cut. Aye dressed immaculate fur the collectin: grey overcoat, white shirt, dark tie, black leather gloves. Still kept himself fit through the weightliftin an the cyclin, which he had done fae way back. Most o his business in the multi involved the recovery of unpaid loans an it seemed he had some business tae attend to in the Gravedigger's house concernin money borrowed an no paid back – whether by the Gravedigger or his wife, nobody knows.

One night he's gettin used tae the multi, startin tae know his customers: who pays back an who disnae; where he should operate as a pair wi another Collecter an so on. At floor thirty he approaches the Gravedigger's house, sees the door is sittin ajar. Walks intae the hall, maybe a bit forward, but still wi that confident policeman's manner o his. Intae the livin room an he's surprised tae be shown in by a young constable, a lad whose face he minds, noddin at him. Then lookin round the room he sees he's stepped intae a scene-of-the-crime procedure: a couple o forensics in white coats are takin fingerprints, peerin aboot wi magnifyin glasses an pickin things up wi tweezers an placin them in wee plastic bags. There's a huddle o police officers at the far end o the room, bent over something. He takes all this in, used tae such scenes until recently. Feelin a wee bit awkward an confused he approaches the group of officers tae explain. It all happens in a few seconds: him enterin through the open door, walkin down the hall, intae the livin-room door, across the floor. The Collector remembers two things happenin next: a big burly officer, presumably the detective sergeant in charge o the case turnin roond, wavin his arms about an roarin: 'Fur Christ's sake! Whaar did he come from? Get that bastard out o here!' an next thing he's starin down at the corpse of a man lyin on the flair, dressed in dark claes, wi black sticky-up hair, glowerin up at him. A shiver through him as he recognises the Gravedigger, one o the lads he used tae pal around wi at school when there wiz a gang o them keen on the bikes, an who he would run intae now an again in connection wi his police work. Rooted tae the spot, starin at the horror in front o him, wi the detective sergeant roarin 'Get him out o here! He can read about it in the moarn's *Courier*!' as two officers manhandle him out the room.

The Gravedigger had murdered his wife.

The Gravedigger's wife had died alone an he hadnae been seen for months.

The wife had murdered the Gravedigger.

The both o them had been found dead.

None of the stories as strange as the one told on the news that night.

The lift engineer carryin out routine work on the windin mechanisms at the top o the buildin, doin a series o checks on the electrical wirin in the crawlspace adjacent tae the windin gear. Only about a metre high – here a man can crawl, or sit up. Him struck by a queer smell of spirit, but no payin too much attention. Movin deeper intae the crawl-space, though, an the smell o alcohol growin stronger. Scannin around wi his headtorch, he catches something in its beam which sends a feelin like a cold knife through him; the light passin it, then returnin an the lift engineer not mistakin the form of a man sittin up in the dark, totally still, lookin straight ahead, the glint o a bottle in his hand. He had seen too much, the beam of his headtorch dancin madly in the blackness as he clattered out the crawlspace and intae the daylight, jabberin.

The Gravedigger's drinkin den, in the crawlspace above his flat. Never goin tae the pub but drinkin more an more over the years, shuttin the hatch in his roof beneath, shuttin out the world an sittin for hours, days, drinkin himself unconscious, time an time again. His wife never knowin if he wiz up there or away at his work, no longer tryin to understand his strangeness; the cold silent man who had never looked at her or spoke to her for years, dyin alone in the dark, her still in that flat today wi her thoughts an memories.

Animals

Dead Hens Mystery

Mystery surrounds the gruesome discovery of the partially burned bodies of six hens on a disused road bordering Dundee's Blackness multi-storey flats.

The bodies of the six birds were found by Blackness Tower resident Thomas Douglas as he walked his dog nearby.

Three black hens had been left at the side of the road – two had their legs chopped off. The charred remains of the three beheaded white hens were lying in the ashes of a bonfire.

'I think the fire was lit on Tuesday night,' said Mr Douglas. 'My wife noticed a smell of burning and heard laughter and squawking. I saw fires in the darkness and went to investigate but I couldn't see anyone.'

Dundee District Council Environmental Health Department has been alerted. A spokesman from Tayside Police advised householders in the area to exercise especial vigilance over their hens: 'Whoever did this could strike again.'

Folk in the tower still kept poultry, a habit brought in wi the early occupants o the multis fae the old tenement way o life. Nowadays only a few faimilies wid hae the wire nettin over the verandah, wi a wee run fur the hens, though in the early days many folk kept them. Back in the tenement days people would hae an area oot the back fur the hens, some faimilies keepin maybe a goat or a pig. The occasional coo wiznae unheard of, an the tenement communities were often self-sufficient in milk, eggs, cheese an butter, wi bacon, poultry an beef sometimes available. The aald man had a picture o his own grandad stroppin a lang curved blade, wi a group o smilin men oot the back wearin bunnets an aprons aa splattered wi blood. The group stood proudly ower a newly slaughtered hog, its forelegs pinioned an its throat slashed above a bucket. Some o the same men could be relied upon tae tak a trip oot tae the Carse wi a crossbow an come hame wi a rustled sheep or twa in the back o the van. Occasionally one o the men wid hae a job up the glens durin the stalkin season an come back wi a supply o venison which wiz aye popular an the same man wid often obtain employment as a beater in the summer an that wid involve a good supply o grouse. Some men kent the best stretches o the Tay fur salmon or trout an a group o lads kept a rowin boat oot the back an were aye handy fur supplies o pelagic fish. Many o the women ran allotments, so vegetables were ayewiz available too.

The aald man's grandad used tae tell of the market that wid be held on a Saturday mornin oot the back in summer, wi folk comin from neighbourin streets. A whole range o produce wid be traded: livestock, flowers, the best o home-made whisky, an shoes made out the expertly tanned hides o locally bred animals. The big skins wid be cured oot the back, flappin aff the waashin lines fur weeks then assembled beh the one-eyed Czechoslovakian master cobbler whaa lived up the stairs fae the aald man's faither. A fire wid be lit an a hail hog wid be turned roond on a spit while street dancers, noseflute players an buglers provided entertainment. Often the day wid end wi a football match involvin all the menfolk fae the neighbourin streets kickin an inflated horsebladder, packed tight wi the singed hair o a hog, over the waashin lines as the settin sun slanted across the tenement roofs.

The aald man told of Rab 'Burd' McFarlane, who eh could just remember fae my childhood in the multi. Seeminly, his aald man knew o him fae the tenements, where he wiz famed as a poultry breeder, specialisin in gigantic specimens, but a stubborn an boastful man, no liked. The aald man minded o his beady ehhs, his lang nose kindo like a beak an his erms aye held doon beh his sides, until he wid flap them aboot an flutter his hands, wi their long nervous fingers, when he got agitated. Rab wiz probably the best poultry breeder in the history o the tenements, an once succeeded in rearin a pair o ostriches fae the egg, kept in an incubator made fae a compost heap in his kitchen. These twa burds bred in turn, an Rab kept the faimily o ostriches oot the back, no somethin that made him any more popular. One night, though, a jealous rival cut the burds loose fae the ropes tetherin them tae the greenie poles, the four o them escapin intae the street, makin a dash fur the main road. One o them panicked an ran over the top o a car, crushin its roof in, the same ane bein hit beh the coal lorry no lang efter. Anither wiz lassoed an the two young anes were shot fae a police car that drew level wi them halfway tae Arbroath.

Rab wiz never the same efter the ostrich fiasco an when his wife Bertha died, somethin turned in his mind. He still had tae go one better than anybody else, though, an his pride an joy in the multi wiz a huge, fat, noisy, ill-natured bugger o a thing which he caad Bertha an kept in a specially constructed cage on the balcony, in anticipation o the biggest eggs in the multi. The only thing wiz, Bertha wiznae a hen. Thon burd never laid an egg in its life. Bertha wiz a cockerel but Rab claimed it widnae be too long till she wiz layin. Once he had an idea in his heid he widnae budge. Efter the neighbours complained aboot bein woken up at fehv o'clock every mornin wi the racket, Rab carried oot an operation on the burd that made it silent for ever. Bertha grew bigger an bigger, wi Rab growin stranger an stranger, braggin aboot his prize hen an no seein what wiz happenin in front o his own ehhs. Thon burd wiz growin bigger than its cage.

A couple o Rab's sisters were up an saw the state o the creature an complained, so he stopped lettin folk in the hoose aathegither in case they the saw the thing. The next anybody saw o it wiz when the aald man's faither went up tae hae a word wi him. The two o them went back a long way, tae when they were laddies in the same tenement, an through his line o work, the aald man's faither had a wey o gettin on wi most folk, an gettin on their good side. The twa o them were sittin in Rab's livin room chattin awa aboot the aald days an nothin seemed amiss until a queer-like shape entered the dimly lit room. Whatever it was moved stiffly across the flair, jerkin mechanically fae side tae side. Rab gave a wee wink, proud-like, let oot a sherp whustle an nodded taewards tha kitchen door which wiz lyin open, the last o the winter sun giein the room an eerie glow. The shape reappeared, set against the light, an the aald man's father could make oot a cage wi a great pair o scaly legs wi big claas stickin oot the sides, movin across the flair taewards him. He made as if tae tak a breenge oot the door when Rab signalled him tae sit doon, coaxin the thing across the room wi 'That's a lass. Good hen, Bertha.' Bertha, Rab's hen, the giant cockerel that had ended up bigger than its ain cage, tae the point whaur it wiz hard tae say whut wiz cage an whut wiz burd. As the great sad beast waddled slowly by, Rab looked at it affectionately, sighin, 'A bit slow on the eggs, but a companionable enough burd, forbye.'

A couple o days later the RSPCA appeared efter bein alerted beh the aald man's faither, took wan look at the creature an contacted the fire brigade, who sent roond a man tae separate the cage fae the burd. If it hadnae been fur diminished responsibility Rab wid have been prosecuted an as it was, it wiznae lang afore he wiz taen awa an put in a home. While the fireman wiz saain the cage aff the sedated burd, the RSPCA man had a quick look roond the hoose an nearly fainted when he found nae bed in Rab's bedroom, jist the great tangled mass o branches an twigs an leaves that Rab had built, linin it wi yarns o wool fae rattled-doon jerseys, insulatin it wi cotton strands aff aald vests. The nest that Rab had been sleepin in these last few months, himself like a great demented burd.

Pets are still as popular as ever, though a different kind o pet seems tae be mair favoured nowadays, wi the trend seemin tae be fur vicious breeds an endangered species. The recently opened pet supermarket up at the shoppin centre taks up three retail units. Most o the ithers are now boarded up an sprayed wi all kinds o graffiti an only the video store, the Morning, Noon an Evening grocery store wi its twenty-four-hour alcohol licence, an the takeaway shop are open an thrivin:

Arabian Nights

This Week's Special: Black Pudding Supper £1

Atomic Hyperlager – 6 cans for a fiver

Other than that, the two charity shops aye seem quite busy wi folk rakin through the racks for things that others have worn. A few folk ye see lookin intae the windae o these shops are people ye remember bein young just a few years ago, but aged an troubled-lookin now, their faces tellin o hard times an losin their way. A lot of the pet-shop business centres aroond the Gun, where's there's always a couple o blackboards chalked up in lurid colours advertisin the latest stock, an lads spend plenty time an money barterin over new arrivals, maybe swappin a Peruvian neon slasher lizard fur a razor-footed swamp macaw, or a purple venom-spitting Mongolian swamp toad fur a white Madagascar stunner crab. The most popular jist now is the Hebridean phantom ray, discovered in the warm waters o the Gulf stream around Barra an the Uists. It wiz only found recently by a couple o boys fae the Gun who go divin up there an they say it's a species still unknown tae science. A few o the lads around here keep ane. Naebody's ever worked oot if it's a big fish or a wee fish, as it's invisible an ye can only tell it's there beh the wee ripples an wake it maks when it's aboot tae kill somethin in the tank. Then there's a silver spark flashin through the waater an the floatin corpse o its victim. All o this interest in pets never guaranteed that youngsters wid be brought up tae treat animals any better, mind, an from time to time an article wid appear in the paper:

More Cat Tortures

Another cat has been found tortured in Blackness, Dundee. Cats in the area have been subjected to systematic cruelty by gangs of children.

A cat found yesterday near the Blackness Burn with a rope round her neck was reckoned by RSPCA officers to have been hanging there for at least two days. Miraculously, she survived her ordeal and has been reunited with her owner. She received 20 stitches to a neck wound.

An RSPCA officer said: 'Many cats go missing in this area. Over 40 have been reported missing in the last month.' A local resident who declined to be named said: 'Last Tuesday I heard wailing and laughter and went out to investigate. I caught a gang of four children, about eight to 10 years old, trying to put a noose around a cat's neck and had to chase them away. Two of them were wearing stout gloves, another was holding a bag and the other one was uncoiling a length of rope. They seemed organised and knew what they were doing.' His wife said: 'Some nights around here the noise is awful. The screeching and yowling drifts up from the Burn on a quiet evening and I've taken to wearing earplugs to get a night's sleep.'

A spokesman for Tayside Police said: 'We are aware of this problem in the Blackness area. It appears to be a trend among youngsters there at the moment. We would ask all cat owners to keep their pets in as much as possible and also request parents to check on the whereabouts of their children during the school holiday period. We are doing all we can to stamp out this unpleasant practice and would appeal to anyone with information to come forward.'

Trance

The history of the place written in the faces o the people an their lives an you could see bairns whose eyes echoed a mother or a grandfather who had lived all their days an nights an years here, forgotten by most but imprinted by the place an leavin a trace of themselves in their own kind in turn. Just a flicker of a smile playin on the lips of a wee lass on the swings, or the quizzical turn of an eyebrow on a lad yed see in the lift, an ye would read the memory of a father or grandmother. Some o the flesh an blood had long gone but lived on in other lives an in the memories an stories passed on an lived each day when a wee one spoke in a certain way, catchin an intonation, or when a teenager moved wi a swaggerin walk that remembered another.

It wiz more than just the people an buildins, though most folk never thought much about the past that lived on in the land around, land that had been lived on long before the Blackness towers went up. Centuries of farmers an peasants an hunters, goin back thousands and thousands of years tae the ancient days of the old Pictish things that would still surface when fields were bein ploughed, or land excavated or blasted where they were layin foundations for the new houses on the edge of the scheme. Nights yed think about yer own family and its sometimes sad history, you sittin in the quiet room wi no lights on, the outside world goin quiet for these few minutes, slowly growin dark. Sometimes ye managed no to think too much about the past then the blink o the lighthouse a few miles off an suddenly yer brother would be back an the sand an the sky an the waves would erase everything in the room. Close yer eyes an it would be more real. Yer own personal history, the past of yer family an yer memories of all others connected wi ye would converge an yed give a shiver as all signs of today wid vanish, you gazin over the river, restless now wi the blur of comin rain sweepin over from the hills of the old kingdom, movin up the flat plains, tae the neat fields in the west, farmed now as then. Then the slow flicker o rain on the window would bring ye back.

Somethin deep within ye loved that time of evenin an that kind of weather, when all signs of today would vanish, only the sound of a distant foghorn moanin out of the greyness. Times like that ye would think of yer aald man an his aald man an all the things they told about the folk you never knew that lived long before, only knowin them from the stories, but those vivid enough in their own way. These people an their lives would live on through their words an your imaginings; as real as some of the people you saw every day, maybe more real. You wid think of ages past when there were no street lights out there, no cars hissin past in the wet, no lighthouse punctuatin the night as ye sat alone for hours in the dark silence. Yer mind would range further an further back, tranced beyond yer own past an into the history of the area.

Slippin into a slow, quiet state like that, hearin in your mind the voices of yer aald man an his aald man, or a voice ye felt ye knew but couldnae place, tellin the stories of the lives of those from the past, near or further back. Some of the memories would be sad, some o them crazed, others mysterious an no makin sense, but comin back tae you again an again, you tryin to work out the sense o some of the things that had happened. Some of the tales ye had heard would mingle with things ye had read an a voice from years ago on the radio would tell its story an merge wi another voice from yesterday an all the voices would weave a memory of past an present, real, imagined an legend, an out of it ye would feel the truth; a great shimmerin history of you an yer people an their lives in this world. Once, lookin out at the mosaic o the lights of the towers, some comin on, others goin off all through the night, the scheme edgin out tae the darkness of the countryside, ye thought how the word history wiz dominated by the word story.

The aald man would tell stories, some that he had heard from his aald man. A funny story. A story aboot love. A story somebody told ye that never happened, but wiz true jist the same. A story within another story. A ghost story about somebody still alive. Stories about things that never happened but could have. Stories still tae be told. Stories were everywhere an all around ye could see an hear narratives: past, present an future. Ye could remember a story yer aald man told ye an you would tell it tae yer own children an never tell it the same way twice an somehow the story took on its own life an it wiz as if the narrative wiz usin you tae make itself real an tae call things into existence through the tellin. These stories ye didnae make up but retold an passed them on to friends who became tellers an the story wid live an grow through them; a voice in a pub or up at the shops or in the bus or goin up in the lift or jist walkin along the road; or a young voice in the school playground or in the playpark at night. Thinkin of early histories ye had heard an read about, ye thought of how all was narrative an how history grew out of the voices of those ye had heard for years. Then yed remember where ye were an shiver in the coldness of that hour an when ye looked at the clock ye wid be startled tae see the time that had passed.

Not far from the multi was the sweep of the bay, sometimes the water lappin quietly against the grey-blue pebbles, echoin itself, sometimes the tide far out over the river. Every summer, older lads would meet others from across the river on one o the great sandbanks at the lowest tide of the year an have time tae play a football match before wadin back over the risin currents, as men had done for decades. Sometimes things would go wrong on the river though; currents, reefs, rip tides an sandbanks had all been mentioned in some of the stories you had heard or in tales of loss in the papers. The names of the reefs an banks themselves tellin of their past: Sure as Death Bank, No Chance Reef, Mad Man's Bank. From an early age the bay an the wood surroundin it had been a favourite place for some. Few people went there but loners or courtin couples who would find quiet green places tae be alone in the spring, screened by trees an leaves, the soft give of grasses a cushion beneath them. Once or twice when ye were young ye would glimpse them through the flickerin curtains of leaves. Ye would hear unaccustomed moans an gasps, seein angles of limbs that made no sense at all; the frenzy like nothing you had ever imagined. Years later an you would come here with a girl, now part of that same game of youth an summer. Maybe a child would pass, like you all these years ago, lookin through the leaves into another world then walkin away, strangely troubled by what he had seen, but himself to become part of the game, in turn.

Comin down from the wood yed reach the bay, its sweep still graceful an natural, its golden fringe of reeds growin for miles beside the coast. Tall, slender, browny-blond shafts, man-high, wi the delicate ferny plumage far above. Walkin into the reeds, further an further in, only the call of a startled bird then silence then the quiet sift of the wind through the reeds. The loneliest sound ye had ever heard an the one ye loved most. The first time ye discovered them ye wanted somethin tae remember, breakin off a sheaf, placin them in a vase in yer livin room for long enough. Lookin over the river from the other side one evenin when ye had walked for hours, ye stood watchin the sun goin down over the hills behind the city, the last light touchin the reed beds, far more than ye had ever imagined, golden at that time of day. Even when ye were little more than a child, something in these lonely places would tug at ye and in later years the hills an the high quiet places pulled in the same way. Soon enough you had learned the names of the winterin birds an ye would know the calls of them, lovin it as it grew dark an still, wi little tae hear but the slow beat o the waves an the curlew sailin over, its bubblin call fadin away, alone, intae the greyness as you turned yer back on the bay, hurryin home before the real darkness came.

Once ye stopped on the way home wi John very late one night or very early one mornin tae look at the sky changin from dark tae grey. In the landscaped area next to the road ye saw a quick flurry an stopped John, who had seen nothin. Years ago the council had planted heathers, shrubs an young trees and now there were wee woods established all over the scheme. On the edge of one, standin in the road nervous but utterly still was one of the small deer yer aald man had told ye lived in the bushes. For an instant it stood there: its nostrils flickered, takin in the scent o humans, then its eye blinked twice an it wiz gone. Pete never believed such things were in the scheme, but one winter morning he thought he had hit a doag wi his electric milkfloat. When he got out tae check his vehicle fur damage he was shocked tae find one o the deer, its delicate legs still twitchin, one side o its face perfect an innocent, the other a mash o bone an gore.

Sometimes yed wake in mid-June, these nights where the sky hardly darkens, unsure of the time, disorientated in that strange summer way when it's impossible tae tell if yev been sleepin for thirty minutes, three hours or nine, the sky givin no sign. Birdsong echoed across the dawn an Venus gleamed above the railbridge, tellin of an early hour. Something in the feel of the mornin said tae stop an wait, lookin over the river, where slowly the bridge started tae disappear. The river fillin wi pale swathes o thick sea fog, only the topmost curves o the railbridge above the clouds, the dark arches coiled like the back of a great sea beast fae the river in its ancient times, as all around the landmarks vanished. No hills, no river, no bridge; the land between the river an you erased in these minutes you gazed from the window. Climbin quietly on to the roof of the buildin, ye saw the slowly risin ocean of white, sea upon a sea. Then the haar driftin in, smoke-like from the river, lifted in endless veils across the breeze. No birdsong now, no sound at all in the muffled whiteness of the haar settlin everywhere below. Yer T-shirt soon clingin wi damp, but it was more than cold that made ye shiver as ye saw the four multi-storeys around yours slowly lost in a drift of white. The sea risin til only the tops of the near buildins stood above the mist, you rapt but wishin it would rise no further, thinkin of goin back down but not wantin to miss the strangeness. You gazin down on the clouds wi the sky above perfect blue. Then the mist settled, risin no more, but stayin for these few minutes that ye always remembered, the sun liftin over the sea of cloud above the river, then shootin low golden rays across the movin cloud. The sun throwin a vast shadow of yerself as a giant, wi a dazzlin rainbow halo pulsin around the edges o the shadow, shimmerin across the layers of glowin white, for miles it seemed. Those moments ye stood, wide-eyed an tranced, watchin as the vast being in front of ye slowly coiled its arms, twisted an danced in time with yer own movements, like a god or a demon, like a dream or a nightmare from yer childhood days.

Dundee Man Stole Gas

A 35-year-old Dundee man, whose incompetent attempts to steal gas in a multi-storey block could have led to a 'large-scale disaster', was today sentenced to 200 hours community service.

Robert McNab, 5A Blackness Tower, admitted that in the early hours of 22 November he attempted to steal a quantity of gas, and culpably and recklessly tampered with gas pipes and fittings in such a manner as to cause severe danger to the lieges. He denied that his intention was to steal the gas, claiming he was 'carrying out an experiment'.

The block's 750 occupants were evacuated and the tower cordoned off. Police officers, the ambulance service, a mobile paramedic unit and fire appliances remained on standby overnight while a team of ScotGas technicians worked around the clock to disconnect the block's gas supply, repair the extensive damage caused by McNab and reconnect the system.

As a safety precaution, teams worked in darkness using headtorches. An unexpected hazard was the numerous attacks by various exotic pets that had escaped through the doors and windows that flat holders had been advised to leave open during the hasty evacuation.

The gas supply was restored to the tower around 8 a.m. and residents, many of whom spent the night in makeshift accommodation in nearby public houses, returned soon after.

Clinical psychologist, Dr Joseph Kay, spoke in defence of his patient, advising that McNab was not motivated by financial considerations or malice, but suffered from an irresistible urge to tamper with gas appliances and electrical fittings. In the past he had lost jobs with ScotGas and Northern Electric and was depressed at the time of the offences. It appeared his predeliction was hereditary, and Dr Kay stated that McNab's grandfather had been involved in an explosion at Lochee Gasworks when 11 people lost their lives in 1953. Dr Kay suggested that his patient attend a course of aversion therapy.

McNab was unavailable for comment.

The Thatched Roof, the Roadside Madonna and the Banjo

The Thatched Roof, the Roadside Madonna and the Banjo

[illegible]

McPhail, Rastus. Beloved brother of Zachariah and Jemima, 'The Black McPhails of Barra'. Peacefully in Lochmaddy General Hospital, South Uist, Wednesday.

This modest cutting, from the *South Uist Gazette* of 14 February 1852, holds the key to a little-known marriage of Gaelic and Negro cultures. It bears testimony to the remarkable and half-forgotten years documented by the nineteenth-century Gaelic historian Iain McIain of Glenelg, who noted in *From The Butt to Barra: A Hebridean Stravaig* his astonishment on hearing:

> a lone banjo above the crags of Glen Dubh picking out the haunting strains of '*Cumha Luchd-Togail Nam Faochagan*' ('The Lament for the Whelk-Gatherers') drifting across the Sound of Barra as dusk fell.

Behind this simple obituary unfolds a drama of slavery, crofting, interracial lust and kelp-harvesting. The slave plantations of North Carolina, the white sands of Barra and the tramlines of Lochee all play their part in piecing together the lives of Rastus, Jemima and Zachariah, 'The Black McPhails of Barra'. Sent by Mary McPhail of Dundee, the cutting merely hints at the intriguing tale our correspondent heard when he visited Mary in her sheltered home in Benbecula Drive. A trim, comfortable living room, with only the Gaelic Bible, a banjo and the articulated skeleton of a guillemot in Mary's display cabinet giving the faintest whisper of her story . . .

In 1782 Marie McPhail, great-grandmother of Mary, stepped from an emigration ship on to the Cape Fear River country of North Carolina, one of many hundred islanders who voyaged to seek their fortunes in that *terra incognita*. These Gaels, hungry for adventure and freedom, fled an increasingly difficult life at the hands of lairds and despots, and constituted the first waves of emigration which broke into a full flood during the notorious Clearances of the next century. On disembarking, she overheard a conversation in Gaelic and, expecting to see some fellow-voyagers, was astonished to discover that the speakers were three Negroes, a girl and two boys, dressed in the full Highland regalia of the McPhails of Barra. Marie's initial surprise changed to deep misgiving when she observed that the Negroes must, in fact, be Gaels who had been blackened by years of exposure to the North Carolina climate. The translation of the letter Marie sent home to Barra conveys her amazement:

> Such blackness of visage I would not dream I could encounter outside, Lord save us, the Kingdom of the

Infernal One himself. The hair itself on the heads of the poor children is shrivelled and crinkled as if by the very fire of hell . . .

The truth was no less strange. The Negroes were, in fact, slaves from the estates of Gaels who had prospered in their new lands and embraced the widely accepted slave culture of North Carolina. Many in due course gave birth to children who were often readily accepted as members of the family, in keeping with traditional island customs of hospitality. Indeed, the names of many of the children are affectionately entered in the family's Gaelic Bible. The Negro children would be brought up in a Gaelic-speaking household and steeped in the language and culture of the Gael. At this point of the story Mary rose from her rocking chair, resourcefully fashioned from the driftwood collected from the shoreline of treeless Barra, and took down from the bookshelf her precious Gaelic Bible. Slowly prising open the heavy pewter clasp with her gnarled hands, Mary pointed to the inscription on the title page, immaculately formed and still clearly readable after more than two centuries:

Born into the union of Obadiah and Jezebel McPhail, beloved slaves of Hector and Flora McPhail of Barra:
On the day of Our Lord 14th October 1770 – Jemima McPhail
On the day of Our Lord 21st August 1771 – Zachariah McPhail
On the day of Our Lord 16th December 1774 – Rastus McPhail

Noting my admiration for the richly grained black leather of the Gaelic Bible, Mary told me how her great-grandfather, Archie McPhail of Barra, had expertly crafted the Bible from the skin of a puffin a few years before he was lost at sea during a porpoise hunt in the Sound of Benbecula.

Continuing her tale, Mary told of the pain of exile felt by her Hebridean forebears in the swamplands of North Carolina and of their heartfelt longing for a return to the bleak, treeless, rain-washed, windswept paradise of Barra. After some decades in their new land, Hector and Flora returned for a lengthy stay in the crofting areas above Castlebay. With them they brought their son Torquil, their daughter Donalda and their adopted children, Jemima, Zachariah and Rastus. The three were slowly bewitched by the austere majesty of the island and entranced by the everyday wonders of Barra; a thatched roof, a roadside Madonna, a puffin. For their parts, the crofters of Barra upheld their proud reputation for fair-mindedness and tolerance and accorded a true Hebridean welcome to the Black McPhails of Barra.

That summer the strong bonds that hold to this day between the crofters of the Outer Hebrides and the Negroes of the American Southern States were formed. The shared love of music and dance which flows through the veins of both peoples flowered in an extraordinary hybrid and before long the blues, Gaelic mouth music, the bagpipe and the banjo were married in a unique form: the 12-Bar Waulking Song of Barra. Sensing my astonishment, Mary took down from her wall the Barra Banjo, made by Rastus McPhail on his second summer on the island. Carefully placing the finely tooled sealskin strap over her right shoulder and expertly running the puffin-bill plectrum over the strings, Mary inhaled deeply, closed her eyes and rendered a stunning performance of 'My Heart is in the Swamplands', a slow 12-bar Gaelic blues, evoking haunting images of tobacco plantations, seal-flaying, the *machair* and racoon-hunting.

Putting down her beloved banjo, Mary told of the profound impact of Rastus McPhail on the traditional music and dance of the Outer Hebrides. His status as a giant of Gaelic culture is confirmed by his single-handed creation of the Gaelic Anti-Work Song. The roots of the development of this singular art form are best left to Fergus McFarlane of Kintyre, an expert in the field of the cultural achievements of indigenous peoples. His survey ranges from the Blue Whelk Cult, where early Christian missionaries produced an eerie music from the shells of the giant blue whelk of the Atlantic coast of Iona, to the Acid Druids of Arran, whose uncompromising music makes extensive use of hallucinogenic barnacles and pneumatic drills. McFarlane devotes considerable attention to Rastus MacPhail and opines:

> The complexity of the Gaelic Anti-Work Song emerges from the diversity of its origins: it draws heavily on McPhail's experience as a slave and the undoubted antipathy to work this engendered. It also grew from the ubiquity of work as a condition of existence on Barra. As always, however, a wholly inexplicable element surrounds the creative process, but what is undeniable is the staggering originality and quality of Rastus McPhail's *oeuvre* and, indeed, his invention of a powerful and subversive genre of song. Anyone in doubt regarding the significance of these achievements need only listen to a sensitive interpretation of such timeless masterpieces as '*Cumha Fear Buana Na Mona* ('Lament of the Peat-

> Cutter') or '*Iesebel Mhor Nan Dorainnean*' ('Big Jezebel of the Sorrows').
>
> *From Ranters to Ravers: Songs of the Islands*,
> Fergus McFarlane (Puffin, 1997)

As a witness to Mary's unaccompanied vocal rendition of '*Cumha Fear – Feannaidh Nan Ron*' ('Seal-Skinner's Blues') the present writer can only accord with McFarlane's generous but realistic assessment. The impact of Rastus McPhail's contribution to Gaelic song and dance spread far beyond the Hebrides, largely through his eventual leadership of the Barra and South Uist Gaelic-Singing Choir. This culminated in the spectacle of a full Gaelic choir, led by a Negro, winning the Gold Medal at the Dundee Mod, with a mesmerising version of '*An Tuathnas Trailleil Agus A'Chroit*' ('The Slave Farm and the Croft'). In addition to winning the coveted award, Rastus also won the heart of many a young lady in the audience, and during his first trip to the Scottish mainland met Mary's grandmother, Dolores 'Dolly' McNab from Lochee, who was to become Rastus's wife and lifelong companion on Barra. Dolly's own talents were considerable; a stunning redhead of tempestuous nature and voracious appetites, her musical ability flourished under the tutelage of Rastus. She was soon to triumph in the Inverary Mod, attaining the Gold Medal in the wholly new category of the Highland Banjo. Dolly's performance, which combined virtuoso musical ability with unprecedented crowd-pleasing movements and gestures, led to the furious resignation of the judge Hector McKinnon from Stornoway, who warned:

> Beware the Wrath of the Omnipotent One – there shall be howling and gnashing in the glens, the islands and straths when the Banjo of the She-Devil comes to the Gaeltacht.'

Later collaborations between Dolly and Rastus saw a Gold Medal triumph in the Highland Dance category when the two led a troop of over three hundred islanders through the Square Sword Dance, the only Mod event ever to be marred by fatalities when twelve dancers perished during the climax of the two-hour performance.

With her engaging personality, her prodigious talents and ravishing looks, Dolly was a popular guest at the many ceilidhs throughout Barra and the Uists where her considerable assets were in great demand. She and Rastus settled happily and their story is one of laughter and contentment amid the, alas, all too troubled Highland past.

Mary's own mother, Martha McPhail, continued the tradition inherited from her parents, and the faded sepia picture on Mary's mantelpiece shows the strong profile of a half-caste islander playing a mouth harp against the stark beauty of a Barra sunset.

My own interest awakened by Mary's tale, it was not long before an uncontrollable yearning took me to Barra. There are few palpable signs of the lives of Rastus, Dolly, Jemima or Zachariah; their legacy lies deep in the hearts of the islanders, immortalised in their songs and their dances. On my last day in Barra, Roderick McCrimmon, one of the oldest islanders, led me to the ruins of a crofting community, the kind all too common in a landscape ravaged by eviction, on the edge of

Glen Dubh. Having walked for five and a half hours through horizontal rain driven by a howling Atlantic gale, I frowned at the old man. Staring impassively back, he led me through a waterlogged ditch at the side of a black house and pointed to the roadside effigy of the Virgin, a not uncommon sight in the Catholic southern Hebrides. Roderick had no English; I have no Gaelic but he smiled gently as I stared, awestruck at the only black roadside Madonna in the Outer Hebrides and calmly whispered two words: 'Rastus McPhail'. Later that day, in the Museum of Island Life in Lochmaddy, I looked on with interest at an expertly fashioned *cas-chrom*, one of the few objects made of wood in the museum. My admiration changed to astonishment and delight when I read the intriguing legend accompanying the artefact:

> A *cas-chrom* or Highland foot-plough, made by Rastus McPhail, from a log of North Carolina pine salvaged from the Atlantic coast of Barra.
>
> Kindly donated by Mary McPhail of Dundee, great-granddaughter of Rastus.

That evening I relaxed in the bar of the Caledonian MacBrayne ferry, gazing wistfully through the rain-lashed porthole at the now distant island. Gathering my thoughts and impressions of this sojourn on Barra and lulled by the motion of the MV *Puffin*, I fell into a light slumber. I was soon startled into wakefulness by the large islander who lurched across my table, upsetting some of the glasses and bottles that had accumulated. There followed a traditional Highland exchange of civilities and whisky, the man enquiring as to my business in the Hebrides. Responding to my own questions, he unwittingly supplied a fitting epilogue to our tale. Alastair McNeill is the fourth generation of his family to work the land and now single-handedly works the same croft as his forefathers, the McNeills of Glen Dubh. In halting English and an unsteady voice he told me how, on a still gloaming, the eerie notes of a banjo lament can be heard, to this day, floating across the gathering night of the Outer Hebrides . . .

Tradition

Like the aald man afore me an his aald man afore him. Caretakers o blocks o multi-storey flats. No just the same area o Dundee either. Naw. The same multi. The multi the aald man's father moved tae as caretaker when they were first built. The multi wi the room the aald man was born in an the same multi eh wiz raised up in. Three generations o caretakers: some say it's in the blood. Now ehm bringin up meh bairns in it. The young lass is three an showin signs o cairryin on the tradition, sittin in the dark scannin the multi opposite wi her binoculars trained on the windaes for hours at a time. Sittin in wi me monitorin the CCTV screens o the new Executive Concierge System in the vestibule in the middle o the night. Like me, fascinated beh the flickerin grey images an the rapid shifts fae harshly lit interior tae dark shadowy outside. Sometimes, an hour o silence broken by a gunshot at the edge o the scheme or a woman's shrieks from much closer an the two o ye would shiver in that dead hour, glad of the perspex security shields ye sat behind wi the dawn slowly fadin up as the end o yer shift drew near. In these days of crime each of the caretakers wi oor own mobile phone an the alarm wi the direct link tae police headquarters. Me an the assistant caretakers workin shifts tae ensure twenty-four-hour surveillance. Five men under me. Thirty storeys, six flats on each landin wi an average o four people bidin in each flat. That's ower seven hundred people at any one time. These multis have been up since the early 1960s. Folk move oot roughly once every five years, so that's a total o near six thoosand folk since me, the aald man an his aald man started the caretakin. An that's no countin the other four multis in the group o five we were responsible fur. That wid make us in charge o the wellbein o near thirty thoosand punters over the years – a good-sized town. All these people wi their struggles an their stories passin through: a suicide fae floor thirty fleein past the windae when yer sittin doon tae yer tea; the night a lassie had twins in the lift; the lad that launched a rifle attack fae floor six on the old folks' home, claimin it had been taken over beh aliens; the time ye were summoned by the police at half-four in the mornin tae assist wi the removal o an ostrich fae the lift. If breeze-blocks could speak there wid be a hell o a stories tae tell.

The aald man's dad telt us that the coffin recess in the back o the lift wiz haunted by the ghosts o all the folk that had ever died in the multi an whose coffin had been brought down in the lift – hundreds o them. He also telt us that the multi wiz actually built on the site o a battle in olden times and that a headless armour-clad warrior had been seen in the lift. Once me an my pal heard heavy metallic clankin fae inside the lift an crept in terrified silence up the twenty-two flights tae his flat. As a boy I minded the time a woman wiz murdered by her husband in the lift efter an evenin in the Gun an my aald man wiz the one who discovered her battered body. People would avoid usin the odd-numbered lift fur weeks after, an some folk swore they heard the woman's screams at the same time o night as she wiz strangled all these years ago.

A game based on the coffin recess wiz later invented an perfected, one of the many in yer teenage years. These were special times in the multi, probably because like everybody else at that time o life, ye were in love with all the risk an craziness that ye wid later expend on women, an if ye knew yer way around a multi, ye could easily find plenty of danger. Goin round an helpin out wi yer aald man ye would find out all the places that were out of bounds an remember how to get in them or, later, acquire a copy o his master key that wid give you an yer pals access to everywhere – lift windin gear, incineration units, the trapdoor that let ye out on to the roof o floor thirty. Next tae the cellars on the ground floor was the entrance tae the waste-disposal unit where John would go. Sometimes, he would go in tae hide from us, other times he would just stand there in the dark for hours, streaks o white light fae the vestibule swimmin across his face through the slatted doors. Once, he decided to hide from us on a Friday night. Friday night an the disposal system in full use; 180 households goin about their business, gettin ready tae go out, clearin up after the tea an waste-disposin. We're lookin for him, shoutin his name through the echoin wind tunnels between the multi an he's dead pleased we cannae find him. In multis there's always antagonism between the tenant who smuggles in a pet an denies its existence, an the caretaker who sees a cat sittin up at an eighth-floor window but cannae prove it's there. Nowadays, wi the exotic species an dangerous breeds there's more acceptance o pets, but in these days the authorities insisted on the caretakers enforcin the no-pets regulations strictly. Human nature bein what it is, some tenants would see the easy way out as shovin the cat down the garbage-disposal chute. John wiz standin under the main chute where all the other chutes empty when a shower o tattie peelins, auld beans, onion skins an a demented cat come fleein down on his head. The first we knew was when we heard an almighty roarin an a clatter o bins an the screechin o a cat soundin like it's bein tortured. The door o the bin recess came hurtlin open an there's John whirlin around, covered in domestic waste, wi a freaked-oot cat hinging doon his back clingin on like a Davy Crockett hat.

Even away back then folk wid keep unusual pets. Accordin tae housin-division regulations ye were expected tae act upon anything the size o a cat upwards. This exempted budgies, guinea pigs, rabbits an so on. One lad pushed his luck, though, an reared an eagle on the balcony o floor twelve. When it started tae fly it caused bother dive-bombin the bairns in the playpark an he wiz asked tae get rid o it. He refused an the aald man wiz given authority tae shoot it an later had it stuffed. The same lad had a narrow escape a few years after wi his snake. The aald man knew he wiz keepin it, but a lot o lads were just startin tae tak an interest in exotic species: lizards, salamanders, iguanas, swamp toads, tree frogs, alligators, snakes an crocodiles were ideal for the multi. The same lads had earlier been breedin mice, rats, budgies an suchlike, so there wiz always a handy food supply. Ye kept them in all the time, they didnae need exercise an the underfloor central-heatin system meant that the temperature wiz jist fine. It could be a bit awkward tae smuggle a ten-foot Himalayan fire python up in the lift, but sometimes the aald man wid assist lads he knew, or come tae an arrangement wi other folk. The lad wi the snake wiz a queer-like fella. Lived on his own, kept himsel tae himsel an never had much tae say in the lift. Wiz aye very regular fur his work in the cold store, though, an took a couple o pints in the Gun on his way home. Like a good caretaker, the aald man noticed he hadnae left fur his work two days runnin, an after makin enquiries in the pub an tryin the door, decided he wid have tae use his master key tae enter an see what wiz goin on. Peerin through the letter box everything had looked normal, but as soon as he went in he sensed something queer. For a start the central heatin wiz on full an as he slowly entered the livin room he saw signs o a struggle – an upturned chair an a standard lamp, still switched on, lyin on the floor. Beyond, the fire python, now twelve feet long, gorged an bloated wi the distinct shape o a man halfway down its enormous girth. The aald man moved fast on this one, alertin the medical authorites, a veterinary surgeon, the mobile resuscitation unit an the two relief caretakers. The three caretakers were barely able to lift the snake, which wiz harmless enough; stunned an huge but a dead weight an it wiz some struggle fur the three o them tae heft it aloft, staggerin an stumblin ower the livin-room flair, layin it in its reinforced glass tank. Slidin the tank out the house an intae the coffin recess wiz easy by comparison. By this time the snake wiz ready tae start digestin him, but they reached the operatin theatre jist in time, an once they cut him oot the snake an gave him state-o-the-art revival treatment, he slowly came roond. It wiz in all the papers – 'Dundee Multi Man Survives Giant

Python Ordeal' – an he still bides in the same flat tae this day. He wiz devastated by the loss o the snake, though, an some say he tried tae sue the medical authorities for no doin more tae save it. He hasnae spoken a word tae anybody since the day he wiz taken oot the snake. Nobody knows if he's traumatised an dumb or still in the huff. Some o the young lads know him as 'Jonah' McGurk, but none o them kens why.

One o the best things about the multis wiz they were built in the countryside on a hill on the margin o the city, overlookin the broad plains at the side of the river, wi the great yellow fringe o reedbeds at its edge. On the clear days you could see across the county beyond the river, tae the river beyond our river an further. Many folk in the scheme moved in for that in the early days, from crowded grey tenements in narrow streets that the sun never climbed above. Here they saw huge skies: sunrises over the gleamin estuary, sandbanks like great low-lyin beasts an the distant forests meetin the beaches on the other side, sunsets burnin over the endless flat plains, the sun droppin slowly in a great blaze behind the hills as ye sat on yer balcony in the golden light burnishin the river. Some folk would never notice any things like that, of course, but ye always knew a fair number wi cameras, binoculars, bird-identification guides an sketchbooks.

Best of all wiz when the last glow died in the western sky, a cold dusk wi the touch of frost late September, when just on the edge of hearin ye would sense the first o the winterin geese, the low honkin growin in intensity as skein after skein would sweep across the darkenin sky, seekin the same roostin grounds as years before, flyin from the feedin grounds from across the river, same as years before. That was one of the best times in the multi – always takin ye by surprise, always the same thrill even after as many years as ye could remember.

Sometimes, in the muffled fog of a grey November, the geese would fly in lower, less sure o their bearins wi no visible landmarks for navigation, sweepin low between the multis, level with yer field o vision. The sound o every autumn of yer life. The weirdest times of all when you an yer girlfriend, alerted by the timeless noise, would use yer aald man's master key tae give ye access tae the roof o the multi – a great space, empty apart from the corpses, bones an skulls o birds or the skeleton of a cat that had crept up there tae die. You an her would lie in the vast emptiness o the roof as the geese flew across in their thousands, above the multi that wiz on their flightpath and part of their memory. Sometimes, a bird would sail close, dark eyes absorbed in its own instinctive world. If the wind wiz in the right direction and the tides were right, the eerie moan o the seals would drift over from the sandbanks as the birds passed. Strange how yed be lyin there with yer girlfriend on the edge of a scheme, tranced, then the sudden tinkle an smash o things bein damaged, or the roarin an thumpin an screamin of a nearby fight would bring ye back.

These were the best days in the life o the multi, though, when the aald man wiz caretaker. Things have grown a lot worse in the time since I wiz first in charge. There's lads on hard drugs in the Gun an the scheme's got a bad reputation in the newspapers the now. No many people buy anything any more: they rob an trade an steal an a group o lads come in the pub at lunchtime maist days an take orders. Anybody needin anything just tells them an they're usually back by teatime wi

Sony PlayStations, videos, Gameboys, mobile phones, Ben Shermans or whatever. If it's too hard tae acquire the stuff from the shopliftin they'll get it fae somebody's hoose.

One o the few growth industries in the scheme is the Dangerous-Dog Breedin – a Javanese trap-jawed slasher hound changed hands fur a grand last week. Some o the arrangements for the organised dogfights centre on the Gun. Sex is the only ither growth area in the scheme. For a while aa the videos in the pub were Scandinavian an American, wi good-lookin models an nice settins. Hard-core porn films starrin folk fae Dundee in their own houses are popular now. Sit down an watch one an ye'll probably recognise a bedroom, livin room or bathroom. Or a voice, a face, a girlfriend or husband. I wiz speakin tae one lad who realised he wiz lookin at his own bedroom then his wife, havin sex wi two men he knew fae the pub. There wiz serious assaults in the paper a day later. People seem tae like the familiarity o the settins an the accents wi folk sayin things like: 'That's a hell o a sehz ane ye huv there, Davie.' It's gone a stage further than that too, an the first I knew wiz when I had tae let the housin inspector in tae look over a house before lettin it out tae new tenants. The folk who had lived there were in danger o bein evicted for their activities an had moonlighted anyway. What I couldnae understand wiz the livin room wi forty chairs set oot in rows, facin a wee stage aw din oot in red vinyl. Then the housin inspector told me that this wiz no uncommon thing and that a group o men were organisin sex shows involvin local men an women in a number o the schemes.

Ours is the only group o multis still standin from the original seven built in the city. One by one all other groups have been knocked down. There's rumours ours is scheduled for demolition by the council as part o the Urban Renewal Initiative an it's hard tae say about the future. It's become harder tae fill the multis wi ordinary people an now there's more an more folk wi problems wi drink an drugs an crime an poverty, livin beside a decreasin minority who have lived there for years in the tidy wee flats they brought up their bairns in. Some o them knew the aald man's father an dinnae want tae leave. A lot o empty property is taken by young homeless folk who squat in it, or young people who break intae it an make fires. One house I was in they had pissed over an electric fire the day before an the reek o burnt ammonia stuck harshly in yer throat and made yer eyes water an nip.

Yesterday I had tae inspect the damage done to the flat that the aald man's father an his wife lived in. Ye thought of the lives o the people who had lived there an all the folk they knew in these far-off days. Some o the ripped wallpaper revealed other wallpaper underneath that ye recognised an it wiz like seein layers of time goin back. Lookin at the big spidery cracks an the smashes in the tiles o the fireplace, ye remembered yer aald man helpin his aald man tae build it all these years past.

The Universal Zapper

There's things tae be said on baith sides an a lot o it depends on the area o the Ferry ye live in like your end's a poor Sky reception area so Cable wid be yer best bet an besides in certain pairts yer no allowed a dish as it's against plannin regulations an anywey Cable's a mair effective wey o transmittin data so that the kind o interference yed sometimes get wi yer dish wid be cut oot. Him ower there wiz moanin aboot the state o the streets efter the Cable boys hud been but it wiz actually the squad fae the Lightin Department replacin the lamp-posts under EEC directives that made the real erse o the pavements an tried tae make out it wiz the Cable technicians tae blame though personally eh think the satellite dishes are much mair o an eyesore an some o the streets are covered in them an it looks like somethin oot *Star Wars* wi aa the hardware hingin aff the ootside o the cottages. Tae be fair though, it's a wee bit o a myth that Cable can dae awa wi the need fur an external aerial aathegither an even wi the current level o technological advance terrestrial TV cannae come solely through yer Cable box as ye always have tae mind that a proportion o Cable capacity has tae be left spare in order fur ye tae look forward wi confidence tae potential future developments like Pay As You View wi yer really up-tae-date films comin in through Cable so yer adverts envisagin a totally aerial-free landscape that will change the face o Britain are a wee bit misleadin an jumpin the gun. Havin said aa that though, eh swapped a lad fae Dundee meh aald satellite dish fur a pair o Siamese fightin fish efter he claimed the dish wiz better than the Cable, predictin that if he had a fault aa he needed tae dae wiz pit the climbin harness on, rope up an get on the ootside o his multi an gie the dish a wee wipe wi his windae-cleanin cloth while eh hud tae put up wi a squad o psychos wi pickaxes an mini JCBs playin Radio 1 aa day stripped tae the waist singin 'Delilah' creatin serious disorder fur a week but him ower there disnae ken his erse fae his fibre optics. A metal box doon the bottom o the road connects up wi a wee grille ootside the hoose an that jines up wi a wee plastic box in yer livin room so fault-findin couldnae be easier also yer phones come through Cable as well an ye can take oot various deals fae basic Cable TV tae TV wi Sports, TV wi Sports an two Film Channels or like mine TV Sports Film an the Internet – aa through yer TV – an fehv telephone lines tae. Ehh. That's me on the information superhighway noo an ehm shoppin an bankin through the Web. A lot o the problems associated wi the early days o Sky are gone wi the advent o Cable like in the aald days when ye had one dish an one decoder so if ye were watchin one Sky channel ye couldnae tape fae anither but now wi Cable there's nae restrictions an at £4.40 a month ye can get an extra box an tape what ye want when ye want an the channels run aa day an aa night an wi the Sky comin through the Cable ye can hiv twelve Sports channels on twenty-four hours a day on twa sets an as fur news ye cannae beat Sky News NBC an CNN an of course yev still got BBC1, BBC2, ITV, Channel 4 an Channel 5 on terrestrial as well as yer radio stations though ye have tae work hard tae keep up wi aa the information about what's actually on but that's where the five magazines ye get as part o yer Cable deal keep ye right though personally eh cannae wait til Digital TV comes oot an ye'll be able tae choose fae about 600 channels although eh suppose Zapper Management'll be that bit mair difficult. Ehh. Zapper Management. At the moment eh hae the six zappers – three fur each TV, video an Cable box an sometimes a zapper goes missin doon the back o the settee or the bairn gets hud o it an presses aa the buttons an maks an affy erse o the programmin. The end nearly came wi me when eh pressed the wife's zapper beh mistake an switched on tae the Discovery Channel an aa o a sudden the Balinese snail worshippers jist disappeared intae a great hissin blizzard o static an eh couldnae switch the set on or aff an when the boy came up fae the TV company he said he'd never seen the likes o it on a Sony so eh decided ehd huv tae go doon tae Argos fur the Universal Zapper. Ehh. THE UNIVERSAL ZAPPER. The next time the wife's mither wiz up she pressed fur the Shoppin Mall Channel. Ehh – kindo like a clubbie book on the TV except it taks ye aboot fourteen hours tae work through, wi each item described in a big cheery voice an showin it fae aa different angles but the wife's mither thinks it's braa an bocht an inflatable rockery fur the balcony o her multi last week. Anywey, the last time she wiz doon here babysittin an she pressed the Universal Zapper the curtains shot open then she tried tae put on the radio an aa the lights in the hoose went aff then the radio came on wi Shirley Bassey singin at full blast an the microwave started bleepin simultaneously wi the garage door fleein open an shut ower an ower again an beh the time the wife an eh got back fae the kickboxin the mither-in-law wiz sittin in the dark gibberin aboot never again. Meh mistake wiz that haein the twa set-ups eh need the twa Universal Zappers an that diz me fur the TVs, videos, Cable boxes, CD player, record player an radio, switchin the computers on an aff, openin an shuttin the curtains, workin the microwave, lockin an unlockin the car, an puttin on the car alarm, the burglar alarm an the security lights.

How? Are ye thinkin o gettin a set-up yerself?

Whut? Ye dinnae believe in television?

Unburied

Three things remained between them.

The suit they shared, hanging behind the door like an afterimage, dark on black. Shoulders tautened by a slender arc of wood, pale as bone, arms and legs drooping slack and dead. The suit that never really fitted his son, never properly fitted him, nearly fitted them both. Always tight across his back, or loose across his son's shoulders, slack after his son lost his way and faded, his father's own flesh and blood, growing thinner, weaker. Then tighter on the father, fitting neither of them.

In its pocket the photograph.

The father's arm placed stiffly on his son's shoulder (wedding or funeral?), a gesture of affection or arrest. The son's eyes calm, these years past, dark hair burnished in the light, his father beside him, face hidden in shadow. All other photographs burned, ripped and lost. He never knew how to smile for the camera. He would rehearse guiltily, straining in front of the mirror, once asking his wife, her smile natural, easy, whether he should part his lips slightly, keep his lips closed, crinkle his eyes. She laughed, shook her head, pointed at the phone book and told him to look up the number of the

Smiling School for Calvinists, where he could sign up for a course of evening classes in smiling.

On its right lapel the strand of hair.

A long fair hair, carefully preened, then the shock of the dark roots, his son's. Lifted between thumb and forefinger from the black lapel of the suit worn at his own son's funeral.

For years his peace was ruined as he lay awake, waiting for his son to come home. His imagination always troubled by the rectangle of light framing the door. An ache nagging and grating at the edge of rest, his mind flickering between sleep, dream and waking.

When will he come home?

Who is he with?

What is the time now?

Where is he?

That light the sign of his son's absence, burning like a slow pain behind the darkness. His body turned away from the door. On the other side the time advancing, precise and digital.

4.23 a.m.

He would wake, troubled and shaking, slowly remembering dreams of his son's death. After the dream, the strange calm, the still room, the blackness, then sleep. His son home now, asleep next door. A book he read long before said that a dream could prepare you for the worst thing that could happen. All these years; the light burning on the stairs up to his son's bedroom outside his own until his son arrived, the light vanishing, then the blackness releasing him. Before that, wakefulness and troubled glances at the rectangle of light around the door and the green digits of the clock pulsing, throbbing. Some nights the peace of an early arrival; other nights he turned over and over, trying to avoid the images blurring the edge of his sleep. Then a door below opened, feet on the stairs, the door in the next room closing quietly. Relief, darkness. Or some nights the pattern of light staying into the morning, the next day, late, promising more haunted dreams that night.

Pale skin, dark hair, grey-blue eyes that never met his for years and would pull away, tearing his heart. The boy looked like his mother. His wife. His son. Years of the boy slowly turning away then leaving.

That light always absent and darkness outside his door now. His bed empty after years of sleeping with another, then sleeping alone. Her body had turned from his, year by year. Too much space and even after so long, the bed too wide. The space to his right, white and cold, where she slept, where he can never lie now. Months after she left he would still imagine the faint scent of her and he would read with his fingertips the indentations left by the press of her limbs over the years, her trace, her body's presence outlined in the emptiness. These impressions could still arouse memories of closeness that would invade his mind, bearing him into sleep.

Sometimes he brought a lover to the empty house and afterwards he would try to sleep, his unknown partner at peace beside him, and he discovered he could no longer share his bed with another. He would lie in the quiet, listening to the breathing of the woman who would leave in a few hours and he would recall the intimacy he missed. His habit and routine had gone; the familiarity he had taken for granted, the art of positioning, embracing, relaxing. An intuitive skill he had learned from sleeping with the same woman for all these years. He missed the coordination, the sense of ease in arms held across one another, the interlocking of fingers, the unconscious adjustments to accommodate a slow shift of limbs, the closeness of breath on breath, the quiet moan that an unexpected touch could awaken. Once it was like this. The rub of her naked back against his chest, his left hand clasping her shoulder, his right arm circling her waist, her hand holding his across her breasts. The slow shift of their sleeping bodies in a telepathy of movement, contours shifting, rearranging.

He still slept in the same bed they had lain in, he and his wife, gazing at their sleeping daughter, three days old, newly arrived from hospital that winter day. Closing his eyes and breathing in, child-smell, the softness and milkiness, the scent of his wife, the mother, mingling with the sweetness of his daughter. Form and function in miniature: hands, fingernails, nostrils, toes. The daughter he had not seen for years, her life now far away and unknown. Then his son, two days old, between them. He remembered his son's eyes when he saw him awaken for the first time: the clearest and most open look he had seen in his life. Beyond the child, his wife smiling back, the same grey-blue of his son's eyes, his daughter's eyes. That Monday he was late for work, staring at the perfection of his son and his sleeping wife. Then holding his son, falling into a slow slumber, the hypnotic breathing of the child, the heart-beat of his wife, the three of them touching one another, asleep.

The sudden chill of recognition the last time he saw his son as he drove past a bus stop in the rain; his son's face pale, unwell, too old. Next, he felt a shock through his heart when he saw his name and the words 'no fixed abode' in the local newspaper and went on to read of a young man arrested for crazed behaviour in a city street.

When his son and daughter were young, before they grew away, he and his wife would take them to the museum, where they would linger over the same exhibit. In the basement, centrepiece of the dimly lit neolithic display, the cist grave. A family tomb found near where they lived, in the style of the area: shallow, wide and flat-bottomed, lined with pale stones, containing the four skeletons. Father, mother, son and daughter. They would stand gazing through the glass of the display at the burial pit, the two adult skeletons sleeping like he and his wife had always slept; the male skeleton behind the woman, echoing the curve of her back and legs. The children's skeletons facing her, the boy echoing the curve of the girl's back and legs. Man and woman, boy and girl; a gentle symmetry. His wife long gone, now his daughter lost, his son in his grave for years.

In later times, he would think about his life and use sleep to escape and forget. He had reclaimed sleep after years of disturbance. Now he perfected slumber, embracing its emptiness. He would fall into sleep in the winter darkness, his face covered, buried beneath layers of bedding as he imagined the weight above him growing, a vast cairn of white, snow falling and accumulating over him, suffocating him as he slid deeper and deeper, further into himself. He would lie on his back in utter stillness, arms folded across his chest like a tomb effigy, imagining the depth of a sleep beyond any he had ever experienced. The snow piled higher above him; he became a dark space underneath, shrinking inwards. The snow drifted, a white grave against a darkening sky. His heart beating more slowly, his sleep deepening. Other times, he could find sleep by imagining himself lying on the floor of a dark forest, great trees towering endlessly above him, hiding the light, shedding a slow flicker of leaves, his body cushioned by years, centuries of leaves layered softly beneath him. A trance of leaves drifted over him, age upon age, a quiet smother of darkness. His body dying under a tomb of foliage, blurring into nature. Later, he would lie on his side in the position of the ancient skeletons he had seen in the cist burials. Crouched on his side with his back hunched, knees bent, he imagined himself under the huge flat slab above him, the earth cold under him, the slow working of time in the darkness of centuries.

Then the shock of his son's sister, his daughter who had gone, returning to the emptiness of the silent house, walking spectrally into the room one afternoon, the thrill of her pale skin, dark hair, grey-blue eyes, the memory of others in her gestures, movements and smiling.

The next few months he spent time with his lost daughter, uneasy and quiet at first after loss and wounding, but talking and living together; the distant young woman he thought he had lost for ever, bringing with her memories of his wife and his son. At first circling one another warily, like frightened animals meeting in a cold space, neither wishing to show a weakness, or worse, a sign of love, their postures of strength concealing pain and vulnerability. Slowly he remembered her, she remembered him. Gradually they became closer then openness: the past, narratives, histories shared.

Harder now to let go of the troubling memory of his son, awakened by his daughter now living in that same room, the returning anxiety of the rectangle of light through his own room's darkness. Then the realisation of her difference; her confidence, her ease with people, her smile, her openness. Like her mother. His son had his mother's looks but his own nature; the boy lost his way and his mother claimed his father's example, his inherited darkness turning to self-destruction. She said to think of the worst that a son could do and the worst that could happen to him and it all flowed through the son from the father, like a fault line in rock, the flaw black and twisted. His wife claimed it was a miracle he was still there and no surprise about her son and his destruction.

After she left, every night he thought of the past and the strangeness of how things that once were the centre of a life could be gone.

Then his daughter's return into his world set in its habits, and her way of making him see things again, sometimes in a startling way. The shock of her looking at the etching he bought for his wife, the one titled *Embrace*, still hanging in its clip-frame in the living room. A densely scratched representation of a couple, two lovers; a man standing behind a woman, one hand reaching across her breasts, the other grasping her shoulder. He thought it an image of love; his daughter said it disturbed her, a representation of brutality and violation, rendered by the nervous cross-hatching that formed their bodies. She pointed at the hollow anonymity of their eyes, blind with hatching, the dark shadows of the features, obscured in the lines that gave them form, bestowing a sense of struggle and terror. His understanding undermined, he thought of what it said of his relationship with the woman who left and of his daughter's reading of the image he had thought safe and fixed.

She brought in her wake a complex trace of revisions and questions, constantly unsettling and blurring the things he had thought of as absolute: himself, his world. She helped him to face things that he had kept buried for too long. One day, he walked into the living room and realised the print had been changed and replaced by a delicate pencil drawing he had sketched all these years ago, freely and spontaneously, showing a child sleeping in its mother's arms. He could remember the evening: his wife's tired eyes slowly closing with the sleeping child in her arms, him working quickly to capture the moment, the drawing completed in ten minutes. His wife had loved the drawing. No sign of time or place; the universal image of Mother and Child. Clothes outlined as drapery, the only details in the hands of the mother, circling the child in love, her sleeping face, her eyes, lips and hair echoed in the face of his son, the face of his daughter, looking at him now.

One memory he celebrated above all others. When they were young they travelled in the old car to the island, the four of them, reaching the crofting cottage just as it grew dark. The next day they looked across the white sands, over the sea loch glittering grey and silver, to the mountains, white-capped like a dream; more lochs and mountains beyond, then the sea and the far islands. In the garden a burn tumbling down from the hills at the back of the cottage, and a tyre swing hanging from the tree. He remembered the children, one on each side of the tyre, as he pushed them laughing and screaming over the burn, the photograph taken by his wife. In the morning they would write their names in the wet white sand and see the letters washed away by the advancing waves, jumping back from the rush of the tide, their young faces cold and beautiful. The boy crying at the end of the holiday, never wanting to come home, wanting to be a farmer's boy and stay with the crofter who had taken him into the hills with his collies, to help him round up his sheep in the bright open days of late spring, the day before he brought the boy and his sister back to the city.

A decade later, he dreamed of the road home. Miles of pitching and dipping on the single-track road, the children yelling at the swoop down to sea level then the small sandy bay. The clearest waters they had ever seen between the island and the mainland: the silver sand gleaming through the blue-green water, seaweed drifting gently. The little turntable car ferry chugging across to the far shore, the mainland with its glens and birch trees, green and swaying. Then the climb out of the glen up the twisting road, reaching the pass between the two mountains; the final lurch over the summit and the suddenness of another mountain opposite; the Scots pines climbing up the mountainside. Tumbling water, loch and river far below. Mountains on all sides and the slow plunge down.

The strangest things she brought with her were the memories. Some nights he would talk with her, other nights he would sit in the darkness alone and remember. Patterns of light around her door recalled the waiting for his son years ago. Listening to the weather and the slow sift of snow against the window in the blackness and his son's face would return to him, through hers. In his life everything seemed connected now and one incident evoked another. His daughter's face lay at the centre of a complex web of memory, delicate and shimmering, trembling with echoes from his past: faces, things said, landscapes, experiences. Waiting for his daughter to come home he would try to picture her face which would blur into his wife's face. Then his wife's face would suggest his son's face: three faces merging and flickering in and out of focus in a composite of the people who defined his life and then its absences. Looking at her, he would see her mother's face from years ago, his daughter wearing her hair now in the style of her mother when he first met her.

He would lie in the darkness listening to the rain crashing against the window and his wife's face would begin to slip away from him, then back into focus, and he remembered.

Would she remember memories differently from him?

Would she think at all about their past?

Could she forget?

Sometimes he couldn't help looking at his daughter through the eyes of others. He would go with her to the nearby pub, where he was still on nodding and talking terms with folk from years ago. He liked it, sitting there talking to her over a couple of drinks, more relaxed now and companionable. He would recall how he had never spent times like this with his son, and how things could have been different, better between them. Then she would catch the sadness in his eyes. He would find it awkward when somebody who didn't know his daughter would leer, a stranger's eyes following her as she walked calmly and easily from the bar, wearing the kind of clothes that young women wore these days. He would see her for what she was now: his daughter, a handsome woman. Once he went into the bar and noticed a noisy group of students in the far corner, young men and women. One turned and walked towards the bar, smiling, her movement poised and attractive. Something echoed in her confident bearing, then the sudden realisation that this woman was his daughter, more like her mother than ever, her hair now long and black.

Once he had walked into the hall as she came out of the bathroom, wet and cold, a towel clenched around her body, rubbing her free hand through her damp hair, her head inclined to the side in her mother's gesture. She smiled; he was quietly troubled. The house now carried the signs of woman, the small intimacies he remembered from years ago and that only a man would notice: a discarded item of underwear beside the shower, a faint smell of sweat mingled with her favourite perfume, the pinkish blur that stained the whiteness of the cotton-wool swabs she used to remove her make-up, the glossy purple kiss where she blotted her lipstick on a tissue.

Months later, when she moved to live with friends, he missed her presence and her signs. Then he readjusted to the quiet of the house. He slept more easily than he had for years, soothed by the darkness, the rain gently driven against the window. He was calmed by the space and the silence, the remembered faces and voices and he thought of a life still to live.

Baather wi Weemin

Hell o a stramash up at the Flenser's Arms last week.

Mair baather?

Blood-transfusion unit, mobile cardiac-arrest, twa police vans, casualty department an intensive-care ward aa involved.

Bad baather. Wha wiz aa there?

Wullie the Tortoise, the Maist Ignorant Woman in the World, Captain Ahab, the Virgin Mary, the Weasel, the Submarine Commander, Musclewoman, the Creator, Barkin Doagie, the One-Woman-Crowd, the Mathematician. An Big Sheila.

Men involved?

Men *an* weemin.

Bad combination. Ye can hae men or weemin. Canna hae baith.

Correct. Ane or the ither. Specially when drink an Big Sheila's involved.

That the same wummin wiz involved in some baather wi a frozen chicken an a Russian hat?

Ehh. Sheila took tae wearin a big black furry Cossack hat in the winter. She wid shoplift occasionally in Safeway's an this time she's wearin the hat an decides tae tak a frozen chicken. Braa big hat. Naebody's lookin. Stuffs the chicken intae the hat an puts the hat back on. Nae problem til she got tae the checkout wi a half-bottle o Navy Rum an a five-litre tin o vinyl matt brilliant white emulsion.

Under the hat?

Dinnae be stupit. Setterday efternain wi a big queue at the checkout an the heatin turned up fur the caald spell an the chicken starts tae thaw wi the waater dreepin doon Sheila's foreheid an nose. Young assistant manager wi the waistcoat, bow tie an concerned expression thinks Sheila's haein a wee turn an he's straight ower wi 'Can I help you, madam? You appear to be in some distress. May I assist in any way?' Shop's got a new Customer Care Scheme in place wi Accelerated Promotion Opportunities fur any member o staff that customers say nice things tae heid office aboot on the Customer Care Freephone Helpline. Well, Big Sheila's no sae concerned wi the assistant non-food manager's career prospects as she is aboot avoidin arrest again.

'Naw – it's awright. It's jist a wee bit on the waarm side in the store the day.'

'Perhaps if you were to remove the hat, madam . . .'

'Naw! Yer awright, son!' an flees the store wi one hand on the Russian hat an the ither shovin puzzled customers oot the road. So that wiz a few weeks ago an Sheila's shoppin in Asda noo.

Last week's baather worse?

Far worse. Crowd o them up at the Flenser's. Men an weemin – Big Sheila an Jimmy, an Avril on her ain – ye'll ken she split up wi Tam efter the giant man-eatin Pacific squid fiasco, an has a wee flat doon fae the pub. Noo, Big Sheila kens Avril an Jimmy go back a lang time an Sheila's edgy aboot this because Avril reminds her aboot it whenever there's a certain amount been drunk. A risky caper, if ye ask me. Anywey, Sheila's in the public bar fur the knife-throwin semi-finals an by the time she gets back tae the lounge, Jimmy's gone. An nae sign o Avril. Beh this time Sheila's seein aa kind o things in her heid an roarin about sortin that bastard oot once an fur aa an she staggers oot the front door even though the Submarine Commander an the One-Woman-Crowd are daein their best tae restrain her. But no. Big Sheila heads straight fur Avril's flat. So she's doon the road an aa fired up an the next thing she's trehin tae batter the door doon, chargin at it ower an ower baalin aboot cheatin couple o bastards an swingin fur thum baith. However, the door steys put an, wi a bit o a crowd startin tae gether beh this time, Big Sheila flings hersel through the livin-room windae in a riot o gless, roarin an blood. An aald lad's sittin waatchin the highlights o Herts versus Dunfermline on *Sportscene* wi the volume turned up fuhl an beh this time Sheila's in a bad wey, craalin aboot the flair, moanin, semi-conscious an lossin blood fest while the aald lad's in a state o severe shock. Wrang hoose. Avril's in her bed in the next tenement an Jimmy's gone hame lang ago.

Some kerry-on, right enough.

Ehh. Big Sheila's a lady maist o the time but gets edgy wi the drink. Her twa lassies are the same, mind. Madonna an Kylie fight ane anither maist weekends an Big Sheila has a fight wi wan or the ither o them at least wance a month. Hell o a baather when Madonna turned up wearin the Rangers strip, an Kylie wi the Celtic strip on fur the Old Firm match on Sky.

Mind you, some say Kylie wid start a fight in an empty hoose an Madonna wid hae a square go wi her ain shadow.

That's Sheila ower there. Big good-lookin smilin wummin wi the neck brace on an the airm in a sling. That's the twa lassies. Seeminly, Sheila tends tae dae that kind o thing mibbee fower or fehv times a year. Looks like Big Sheila's gone ower far this time, though. Some o the regulars hud a whip-roond fur the Anger Management Course an if she refuses it wance mair that's her barred fae the Flenser's fur life.

Fall

The strangest game I taught the children was the Fall. Twice, three times a year I would lure the youngest. A rare thing, seen by few. The ceremony on your doorstep could sometimes be the most beautiful, yet stay unknown. Switch on TV to see a dance from some unheard-of land where a girl, tranced and painted, plays Bride of Death. An expressionless youth lowers himself on to a bed of broken glass, or slowly moves through fire, the uncanny calmness on his face, arms blurring in slow arcs, flames dancing around naked thighs. The Fall was as strange.

Teaching one group of children ensured that another would soon learn; a tradition of the very young that I controlled. After a death I would learn the coordinates of the body, the sprawl of limbs smashed on the concrete at the foot of the building. As I started chalking the outline, the children would quietly arrive; little friends and brothers and sisters holding hands, staying a safe distance, approaching then retreating and spectating uneasily as I smiled at them, skilfully delineating the pose of the recent dead. The children would gather, not wanting to stay, not wanting to go, repelled by my own ruined body, the damage of my broken symmetry, my form twisted as any that I drew. They would come closer and stay, pulled by the soft lull of my voice and the smiling profile of my face, young and beautiful still. When undisturbed I would keep drawing within the outline, my skills growing more expert, until every feature of death was swiftly completed, the children held, fascinated.

A raucous shout from an adult voice summoned a child from the press of the crowd which concealed my work. The children vanished, the space decorated with a bright geometry of limbs, heraldic colours outlined in gold. Hours later, a caretaker wearily scrubbed as I looked down, observing the spectral glow of the shape which, like the other images through the years, would stain the ground and the memories of the children for ever.

Only in the multi-storeys was my game ever played and this made sense. Every year I could predict the two or three deaths: I knew the condition of the vulnerable who lived there. Late December, January, February; the time the lonely or desperate would choose. I would think of her sitting there, the first year alone with her child, the partner she barely knew vanished from her life; I knew of the divorced or the recently redundant or of her surviving alone in the flat that nobody would ever visit as long as she lived, in these dark times of cards, adverts and tinsel.

The game carried the same stirrings of fear and arousal remembered from all these years ago when we played Best Man Dies, on the steep grassy hill behind the municipal tennis courts. The casual executioners would gather at the foot of the slope, controlling an imagined weaponry of fearsome potency and sophistication. The prisoner upslope would request death by pistol, grenade, scimitar, shower of arrows, flame-thrower, stoning. I would respond with a slow, stylised mime to my chosen death, my protracted dance of agony always winning, its theatrical abandon followed by a solemn, silent spell of stillness, my body broken and contorted in my mind while my executioners, all boys, would inspect my corpse, lingering over my disordered dress and abandoned limbs, their breaths rising. Afterwards, they would reluctantly agree that, once again, the authenticity of my imagined death had won.

Sometimes the cruder technology stimulated a more dramatic death: a hammer assault, a frenzied razor attack or a slow strangulation could inspire the most tortured mime. Our eager imaginations would find stimulus in the films of the day: Charles Laughton as Quasimodo, pouring boiling oil over the screaming invaders below from the gargoyled heights of Notre-Dame, the agony of Kirk Douglas in *The Vikings* as the talons of a hawk tore the living eye from his face, or Tony Curtis thrown to a howling pit of slavering wolves in the same film. Local events would fire our minds: the time when an inmate from a high-security mental institution broke out to rape then batter to death a local woman, leaving her ravished body in the field on the perimeter of our scheme, to be discovered by one of my friends walking to school the next morning. At lunch break myself and another girl hurried to the scene of the murder, the exact spot covered now with a blanket and two policemen posted while another inspected the ground. That afternoon we were scolded by our teacher when we arrived late in school, breathless and secretly elated.

My body would stir with a quiet thrill as I examined the grainy black-and-white scene-of-the crime photographs reproduced on the rough, fibrous paper of the American pulp magazines I saved my pocket money to buy. I pored over shadowy tableaux taken from police files, showing the glamorous victims of night sex attacks; violated women with their clothing disarrayed, limbs thrown in chaotic angles, their final moments of terror captured in the crude flash of the camera for my entertainment. The illicit thrill was charged by the black rectangle placed over the victim's eyes, a black mask bestowing anonymity, erasing identity, transforming her into a blind object of desire. This allure was intensified by the forbidden rituals of USA mail order and its paraphernalia of zip codes and shipment charges. This invested items like X-Ray Spex (always advertised by a man secretly leering at a buxom woman dressed in black underwear and stiletto heels) with an exotic aura of unattainability. Elsewhere in these magazines, among the thrilling cornucopia of Americana, hidden away in cramped small ads in overinked type, were box numbers to contact for Genuine Nazi War Atrocity footage, Live Autopsies and Animal Savagery films.

The game of Best Man Dies by now provided less excitement than before, and occasionally I would allow one of the boys to win, my interest shifting to the older girls I watched playing tennis, arms thrown back in that frozen moment of service, the billowing pleats, a flurry of white frill and flesh, followed by the ache in me, the mystery. The game and the magazines came to mean the same: the closed eyes, the inclination of the head, the facial expressions frozen in an unreadable zone between pain and desire, the angle of spread-eagled limbs and the disturbed clothing. Decades later, echoes of these thrills returned when I first knelt over a victim of the Fall, underneath the sixth-floor balcony she had plunged from during a New Year party, her eyes half-closed, her party make-up blurred on her young face, her glittering dress wet, clinging.

Soon after these deaths, the police would arrive. Occasionally, suspicious circumstances brought colleagues from the forensic-sciences department and once a mobile incident room was set up in a police caravan trailer, centre of the murder inquiry. Sometimes the outline of the body was chalked in around it shortly before its removal; sometimes the body would be too far-flung or badly broken. One body, now ruined and damaged for ever, survived the Fall. Certain areas of the tower were favoured for death, and it became clear which suicides had considered their end and studied the optimum vantage point, and which ones had impulsively leaped from any apparently lethal height. In my mind I would rehearse my own Fall. I knew the areas favoured for a perfect death: the unobstructed plummet from the highest point on the roof, the step into freefall. Access was limited, but those who knew and were determined could emerge on to the vast windy expanse of the tower's roof. Some dived into the wind tunnel that separated the building: once I saw a hurtling body tumble crudely from one side of the narrow canyon to the other, banging and scraping off the rough harled stones, wall to wall, landing shredded and broken three hundred feet below. These were the worst to see; others would face the vast car park and plunge to uninterrrupted death. The girl I found there that New Year lay in strange repose; one of her arms theatrically outflung, the other twisted under her broken back in an impossible posture, her lips parted, her make-up spoiled, her young face tainted and beautiful.

Sometimes working with the children could bring strange results. They would shift as I spoke to them, checking over their shoulders, warned by mothers and fathers. Some would sidle away but return, troubled but reluctant to leave as I started to draw, more swiftly than ever before. My memory stored the details of all the deaths from the past: the configurations, the coordinates, the gender, the outlines of all the dead in their chaos of poses. Inscribing image after image, the catalogue of the dead from the years materialised; outlines intertwining, overlapping in a scrawled inventory, each space labelled with a name, a date, an age. I would guide some of the more eager hands and soon the more confident children, under my direction, would chart the shape around the points indicating head, shoulders, arms, legs. Afterwards, the children danced in a mimicry of death, twisting their bodies into the templates of the dead. Sometimes the game lasted minutes, always ending with a harsh voice summoning from above, the children fading, their abandoned diagram waiting for the morning.

The parents would soon forget what their children remembered. The blurring of feet over the waxed images left a smudged palimpsest, a mesh of hues glowing into one another after a night of rain, readable still to the memory of the children. By afternoon, a crudely chalked phallus, scribbled pubic hair, the ballooning of impossible breasts and the slash of a vulva had created an obscene Resurrection, the dead coming to life in an orgy of crude scrawlings, at once innocent and knowing. Early evening and the games of the children had erased the marks, now bleeding into a mist of colours.

All these years I had remained fascinated by the Fall: Best Man Dies was a drama of arousal, shadowy and half-understood, awakened in the instant of thrashing to the ground in slow motion. Years after, the sudden shock of a body hurtling in a blur past the window excited the same shiver and my first sight of the disarrayed form, the frenzy of police and ambulance, inspired a new and unnameable thrill. Soon after, I returned to draw the young woman's body and hours later the children played, shrilly arguing over who would lie in her shape, after miming her death in a slow dance.

From my vantage point at the loneliest height of the tower, I could discern the faint tracery of marks below, a sudden gust catching my breath, ruffling my long dress, sending me forward in a lurch I could barely arrest. A small group of children had gathered in the car park. One of them looked up from the shapes they played amongst and saw the figure poised at the edge of the building, understood and waved in sudden, excited anticipation. I gazed down at the children, still and silent, a dark angel.

The late-afternoon sun dipped behind the darkening hills, flooding the river with an orange light. Beyond the near hills, the forest, black and dense, climbed towards the distant mountains, cold grey with a tracery of white on the higher tops. Such beauty a backdrop for the perfection of my Fall.

The tingling thrill in the pit of my stomach, the hurtle of the sky, the tumble of the river, the ground plummeting upwards in a grey blur, the crowd of children parting, my shape joining all other shapes from the years.

A flicker of darkness then light then darkness then the rough grey of the concrete of the car park, the gleam of a thousand crystals faceted from the smashed screens of robbed cars. The crowd gathering, the pain searing and the light flickering. A vision of a body bent in ruin. Young voices then a child drawing.

Fear a Bhata

The streets, lined ten-deep wi people, still an quiet. Nae sound at aa, bar the gentle slap o the sea lappin aff the hulls o the rowin boats, a stray wind moanin round the flensin shed, rattlin a loose slat or twa in the eel-smokin huts, an a few folk no managin tae hold back a sob. Folk sittin on rooftops, bairns wi their heids stickin oot skylights an some o the young men standin tae attention on the crow-stepped gables o the limewashed fishin cottages, wi a gull's-eye view o the funeral o Boat Rab. The cortège slowly windin its way down Flenser's Brae, intae Boat Lane, the rowin boat containin Rab shouldered by the Submarine Commander, the Creator, the Maist Ignorant Man in the World, Big Sheila an the One-Man-Crowd. The procession solemnly passin, Rab lyin there in his favourite boat, *The Princess of the Kelp Harvest*, his huge hands aa chapped an rough wi the weals an scars fae countless tussles wi hook, beak, tusk, claw an scale, folded neatly ower his chest, clutchin a picture o the Admiral, his beloved Hebridean seal-huntin hound. Rab's entire body up tae his chest wound in layers o densely woven fishin nets, his neck an shithers garlanded wi a ruff o glistenin kelp. The nets fastened thegither wi the gleamin white jaws o small fierce marine creatures, spangled wi crustaceans, studded wi barnacles an anenomes wi delicately wavin tentacles. Occasionally, a crab wid scuttle across Rab's torso tae attack a prawn or a shrimp. The great purple masses o broken blood vessels on Rab's nose an cheeks now muted, his bloodshot eyes closed. Rab had never looked as young as he did that day, lyin dead in *The Princess of the Kelp Harvest*, covered in nets, marine animals an seaweed.

As the cortège approached the Seal-Flayer's Arms, the Submarine Commander struck the openin notes o 'Fear A Bhata', pure an clear that October mornin, performed on the aald battered trumpet that Rab used tae play tae the crew of *The Princess* as they returned on a brisk south-westerly efter a good night on the fishin. A slow dawn comin up ower the Tay wi Boat Rab, trumpet aloft, sihouetted at the stern, wi maybe 'Spanish Eyes' or 'South of the Border, Down Mexico Way', driftin over the waves, the sky clearin from dark tae grey tae light over the wakin village. Sometimes, comin hame wi a big catch, 'The Cucaracca' or 'She Wears Red Feathers and a Hula-Hula Skirt' wid ring out across the river, rousin the town from its slumber, the boat glidin through the waves, the Admiral howlin a duet wi Boat Rab's trumpet. The Submarine Commander claims that once, in the middle o 'Stranger on the Shore', Rab lowered the trumpet fae his lips an the doag continued howlin, unaccompanied an note-perfect, motionless at the prow o the boat, its great silver heid tilted back in the moonlight, mair mythical beast than real doag.

When the Admiral wiz on the go Rab an the doag were rarely seen apart, an some lads say the twa o them had an uncanny understandin. Some claim the beast had the power o speech, an also that it had the gift of the Hebridean Second Sight. Boat Rab telt the Creator that the doag's great-great-grandfather wiz bred by Blind Hector, the wan-legged banjo-playin visionary fae South Uist. The Mathematician claims he once spent a night at Rab's, sleepin in a porpoise-skin coracle on the flair o the livin room, a few years after Rab's wife Jeannie passed awaa. He claims he heard two low voices in the middle o the night arguin ower the best wey tae flay a seal. Ane o the voices he could recognise as Rab's sayin:

'Personally, eh wid aye mak the wan incision wi a flensin knife jist below the snout, an peel the skin aff in twa equal sections.'

The other voice, low an growlin, he couldnae identify:

'Naw. That's fine fur a porpoise, but fur a seal what's required is a twa-centimetre groove cut roond the neck wi a freshly honed halibut gaff, an the hail skin comes aff in a wanner, flippers an aa.'

A spirited discussion ensued, encompassing puffin-flaying techniques, guillemot-trapping and gannet-strangling. The Mathematician, intrigued, rose from his coracle, carefully picking his way through the oars, creels, seal traps, harpoons and flensing knives, past the blubber-curing racks in Rab's lobby. Through the smoky glow of the whale-oil lamp, the Mathematician could discern the smiling, relaxed figure of Boat Rab, reclining in his rowing boat, smoking a pipeful of kelp, the Admiral swinging gently in a drift-net hammock, its head noddin, its great paws folded over the side, idly chewin a kipper. Accordin tae some, the doag's gift o the Second Sight wiz responsible fur preventin Rab fae goin tae the fishin the night a giant man-eatin Pacific squid drifted off-course fae the Gulf Stream, attackin a rowin boat wi the loss o three men an twa women. Some maybe exaggerated stories aboot the doag, but eh personally witnessed its behaviour at sea, the beast sniffin the air a couple o times an then wi a sweep o its paw signallin tae turn the boat aroond, an minutes later bein in among shoals o herrin, thousands deep. That night there wiz so much fish in *The Princess of the Kelp Harvest* that we had tae fling the Admiral overboard as ballast an it swum ahead o the boat aa the wey tae the harbour, its great back glowin in the eerie pink light, a slow night mist risin fae the sea as Rab struck up the openin bars of 'Red Sails in the Sunset'.

Rab's dyin wish wiz tae be buried at sea near Mad Man's Bank whaar he had laid the Admiral tae rest efter it exploded in the middle o the night fae its condition. Rab had his wish granted when he wiz gently hoisted overboard in a specially devised sarcophagus made by the Creator out o two equally sized rowin boats, joined tae one another wi nails, tar an caulkin.

The Creator's latest project is the Boat Rab monument: the life-size statue he's carvin fae a great spar o Hebridean pine fae the forests of South Uist, mysteriously washed up on the foreshore an lugged up tae the Creator's Research Bureau by Big Sheila an the One-Man-Crowd. The smell o wood-shavins, paint, rum, kelp smoke an varnish; the sound o planin, cursin, sawin an Latin-American trumpet music as the likeness of Boat Rab slowly forms at the hand o the Creator, ready tae take its place lookin over the river, for ever searchin out the smell o the sea . . .

Afterglow

The sudden thrill o voices, ringin across the emptiness, across their fields an streets, across the remainin light, their cries echoin up tae the room in the tower from decades away. The sun a slow blaze at the world's edge, long shadows fingerin from the west. The windae now a block o gold, the far wall a rectangle of fire. Day fadin intae dusk an the distant calls o the bairns now focused an desperate, searchin for an endin tae the game before bein called in for the night. Sometimes the finish of the game in urgent silence then a child returnin tae the tower, face lit from within: breath quick, silent now, movin in the quiet o his own world, dazed from the intensity of play. Lookin out at the shadows stretchin across the deserted playpark at the same roundabout played on in another life, circlin then slowin, its burnish of cold iron a slow flicker caught once or twice in the last gleam, before it stops.

The swoon: the light-headedness like the aura before a trance. Shadows across the mown cornfield: limbs tinglin an body fallin, in motion an drugged from the exhaustion, head light an spinnin, arms stretched wide, startin tae float, leanin backwards, the world a birlin shimmer an everything goin intae slow motion then the dry scratch o the stalks, the raw earth scent then each windae in the tower a flashin gleam of amber then everything a blur. Frightened an thrilled at the strangeness of the world: blood pulsin through veins, the rhythm poundin through the head, the depths of redness behind closed eyes then openin them suddenly an the glory of clouds driftin past, slow an edged in gold.

In summer the corn turnin from green tae yellow, the quiet sift of it against limbs an the soft hush of it under yer body in later times lyin with a girl, like the older boys seen years before when we looked on as children, intrigued but disturbed at the desperation an urgency of what we saw: the writhe and abandon in the deep seethe of the field, the strange distant ecstasy in the eyes of the teenage couple, as if in some faraway space an time. Years later playin their game, yours now, in the same field under the same sky in the drowsy stillness o summer wi jist you an a lass in the far corner near the woods away from all others. The cries of the younger ones driftin across the perfection of late afternoon as the two of ye lay in afterglow wi the larks climbin higher an higher, their mad song spirallin further an further above, still echoin in yer mind decades later.

Even then, the quiet arousal o fear an destruction: the temptation o the field, its rustlin dryness after rainless weeks at the edge of boredom in summer holidays that suddenly felt too long. The restlessness of teenage years an already the pain an bitterness of memory an things recently treasured that ye now wanted tae destroy. Growin older, an play blurrin intae danger. One match lit an tossed then three boys watched, speechless: the hiss an flicker, the crackle o the shrivellin stalks, the halo of flame glowin around the blackened heart of the corn, the tremble of air above the field, the surge of fire, spreadin. The thrill of watchin from the tower as night fell an flames raged across the sky an through yer mind as you dreamed beside an open window, the curtain billowin like a ghost, the scent of fire driftin through yer sleep.

Funny how games of fire were always loved, especially wi Pete an John involved, as they could usually think up something mad an excitin an dangerous. No long after his match set the field up in a sheet o flame, Pete thought up a game that kept us occupied after the darker nights set in, turnin autumn taewards winter. A few years after the coffin recess had been locked an some months after the burnin o the cornfield, Pete invented the game we played for a few weeks before the police moved in. The game wiz simple but clever an spectacular, wi the edge o danger we loved. It took somebody as ingenious as Pete tae recognise the creative an destructive potential o the steel vacuum-cleaner tube that he stole oot the hoose, explainin tae us how it could be adapted fur use as a highly effective rocket launcher, tae direct giant Guy Fawkes rockets wi pinpoint accuracy at various targets. John christened the game Hoover Attack an the three o us terrorised the corporation buses on the Number 17 route next tae the cornfield for a week that November. That wiz after we had perfected oor technique by firin at windaes, fierce doags, people ye didnae like an eventually cars. A taxi wiz involved in an accident when its driver lost control an swerved intae the path of another car, followin a rocket bouncin aff its windscreen in a great fantail o sparks.

Things took a more serious an committed turn after a description o the three o us appeared in the local paper an John suggested we change oor appearance. Partly for disguise, partly tae hide in the dark an partly tae gie us the right kind o attitude an discipline, we took tae wearin snorkel parkas, camouflage troosers an black fourteen-hole Doc Marten boots, callin oorselves the Active Service Unit. Pete wiz now the overseer o the operation an he wid give out instructions, selectin targets an strategies. I wid kneel wi my right knee on the ground, cradlin the long cold shiny length o the Electrolux tube over my right shoulder an positionin it wi my left hand. John wiz responsible fur insertin the rocket intae the front end an placin a lang taper some distance up the back, dependin on the length o the rocket an the distance o the blue touchpaper within the tube. He wiz also in charge o the acquisition of the rockets. Pete stood back and estimated angles, distances an time o travel, afterwards givin the signal tae run after spectatin the result for an appropriate duration. On a couple of occasions Pete brought his camera along tae record the result, somethin I wiz never that relaxed about. When Pete gave John the order tae light the rocket we wid all go tense. A slow curl o blue smoke wid float fae the rear o the tube then a fizz o sparks followed by a great sudden whoosh o orange, the three o us chokin in the blur o reek, eyes nippin an throats catchin as yer rocket surged intae the night, zoomin taewards its target. Pete issued each o us wi a Dundee United scarf which we wore over oor mouths an noses durin launches. John, whose eyes were more sensitive than ours, took tae wearin his aald man's weldin goggles as an extra precaution against the flash an smoke.

Things eventually got out o hand when John persuaded his big brither tae steal a giant rocket fae his work at the Municipal Parks Depot where the Corporation stored the equipment for the local public fireworks display an bonfire. John arrived wi a three-foot rocket stuffed inside his parka an when eh saw it at first eh doubted if it wid fit intae the tube. Pete wiz elated, though, an soon we were emergin fae the darkness o the field, takin up oor position at the side o the bus route, launchin the rocket intae the open staircase at the back o the Number 17. Yer rocket wid normally fizzle oot no long after its initial impact, but this type wiz designed fur open spaces, displayin the range o features stuffed in its nose-cone efter shootin a hundred feet up in the air. The rocket hurtled intae the luggage compartment o the double-decker, explodin in a blindin flash o purple, turnin tae green then pink. In the few seconds between each colour there wiz a high whinin howl followed beh a deafenin screech accompanied beh a series o staccato bangs as if somebody wiz tryin tae shoot a fighter plane oot the sky. Efter the rocket had spent itsel, a huge plume o blue smoke drifted out the back o the bus, trailin fur a hundred yards alang the street. Seeminly, the conductor had radioed fur help an a fire appliance arrived wi a police car shortly afterwards as we watched fae the dark o the field. Luckily the bus wiznae busy an a couple o firemen wearin breathin apparatus were able tae go upstairs an bring doon two drunks, wan stunned an the ither gibberin. The next day the paper carried a picture o the bus, aa charred an blackened, wi the grim-faced conductor an driver glowerin under the headline:

Rocket Hoodlums Terrorise Bus Route

In a wey, it wiz lucky that the police caught up wi us then, as Pete had persuaded John an me tae steal the hoover tubes out oor hooses too, so he could experiment wi what he referred to excitedly as 'Triple Fire Power'. My aald man, who had read the bit in the paper, wiz suspicious when he noticed the hoover tube, usually bright an gleamin, aa cloudy on the ootside wi smoke stains an smellin o guns when I put it back in the lobby cupboard. Efter he contacted the police, there wiz panel hearins, social workers, assurances o good future behaviour an talk o a session wi an educational psychologist fur Pete.

Beh fourth year, Pete had become somethin o a celebrity in the school: hated an feared by most o the teachers who never felt easy wi him in their classes, but popular wi his fellow-pupils, who were ayewiz on the lookout for what he would come up wi next. It wiznae lang before Pete wiz in further baather over his fascination wi fire an this time he wiz suspended fae school fur a couple o weeks efter aimin a great jet of meths oot a syringe intae the flame o a Bunsen burner when the chemistry teacher went intae the wee room at the back o the lab fur his cup o tea. A sudden squirt o meths at the Bunsen an a great lick o flame hurtled up the back of the science room, settin a lassie's blazer on fire. The teacher heard the noise, rushin intae the room tae find us rollin her aboot the flair, Pete whooshin a fire extinguisher all over the screamin lassie.

Pete seemed tae enjoy aa the attention o the inquiry that followed but his last trick in the school wiz one mornin interval when he set fire tae chairs an desks fae the jannie's storeroom. Wi a combination o lighter fuel an a couple o matches he soon had wee tongues o fire leapin up fae an aald easy chair oot the staffroom. The fabric of the chair smouldered and smoked wi black reek, meltin an oozin a thick dark slime as a yellow flame slowly grew an coiled above the ripped seat. The small group o pupils soon swelled intae a crowd attracted by the pillar o fire an smoke billowin above the bike shed. Those nearest started tae feel the heat on their faces as the foam turned intae a thick black bubblin liquid that threatened tae splutter over those nearest. Some at the front tried tae move away but were forced forward by those pushin fae the back. Pete, knowin he wiz on his last chance, panicked an took a run at the chair, kickin it on its side. As he jumped and stamped on the overturned chair the flames lowered. His poundin feet shot black scraps intae the air, swirled by the breeze into the faces of those nearest. A wee yellow flame darted around the underside o his Doc Martens as the unattended chair leaped back tae life. Pete hopped then rolled over on his back, makin frantic cyclin movements in the air as the flame from his rapidly meltin sole licked over the toe of his shoes and into the turn-ups o his jeans. Most o the crowd just stood an stared as me an John started tae flap oor blazers against his legs as he flailed aboot kickin jist as the rector arrived. Pete wiz taken away in an ambulance an never came back tae school after that day.

Personally, eh only once ever sustained a serious injury durin a game. For about a year there wiz a craze fur bikes an ye wid ride yer bike in the space inside the lock-up garages, their doors facin one another in a ring. We soon got bored o racin round the circle an decided a better idea wid be tae lift the bikes on tae the ashphalted roof o the lock-ups. Vehicles wid enter through a gap in the circle, about the width o a car an a half. At first the race wid start at one side o the gap an two or three riders wid pedal madly in a counter-clockwise direction on the roof, screechin an judderin tae a halt just before the gap at the other side. Once, John lost control o his bike efter his rear wheel touched the gutter o the inside lane, an came crashin down on top o a car that wiz slowly reversin intae the open door o one o the garages below. By the time the furious driver managed tae emerge from the boot o his damaged car we had vanished. John's recklessness led tae a modification o the game; the object bein tae try an build up enough power tae hurtle across the gap an land safely on the other side. John attempted it twice, succeedin both times by keepin close tae the inside edge, where the gap wiz at its narrowest. The only ither person tae attempt it wiz me, after some technical advice fae John about positionin yer wheels correctly an liftin yer handlebars at the right moment. The blur o sky as ye picked up speed, cheerin voices, then the freefall of sailin over the gap but the trail of the wheel jist catchin against the edge an the scrape an gash o the harlin against yer side an shoulder then the blankness on hittin the concrete: everything slow an hushed, the circle o yer pals bendin over, silent an starin.

Voices, closer now. Watchin them return in the twilight, the game ended until tomorrow. Reading in their faces the signs of a narrative still tae be told, still tae be written: the face of a child to grow happy an kind an able tae love, the face of a child soon tae grow dark an bitter an taint the lives of others. Sometimes the signs of both in one unreadable young face: the possibility of love, cruelty, happiness, destruction. The face of a nurse, the face of a teacher, face of a criminal, victim, poet, abuser. The years tae come sometimes traced in the shadows of a face, already troubled or smilin, the mystery of a life yet tae be lived in darkness, in light.

Years

Walking above the car park, slowing to look at the top of the mountain glowering over the corrie gashed with ice and snow, the summit distant and perfect. Climbing straight up the front would once have been the way taken by the two of us. Now all walking's done alone. The long walk ahead, much of it in sight now. Through the young plantation pines, far taller today than I would have guessed, remembering the times before they were planted in the open of the glen. Through the mature wood, breath smoking in the cold stillness, breathing the only sound then the feathery thump of snow from a springing branch above; underfoot, years and years of needles, green to golden to brown, the soft give below. The trees halting in a line on the opposite side of the glen; between the bealach with the lip of the cornice always hanging over at this time of the year, the burn falling, white water between the tumble of rocks breaking through snow, flanked by the scree, later meeting other burns from other corries, settling into the deep surge of the river further down. The zigzag of the track up the mountainside, far up to the bealach, disappearing, then the climb from the col up to the plateau, always longer and harder than it looks. Beyond, the sky; unreal blue of a postcard. Everything still and cold: blue of the sky, white of the snow, silver-grey of the frost, blue-grey of the rocks, green-grey of the pines. Slowly climbing and looking down at the car park, deserted except for mine. A strange enough Hogmanay and a strange millennium celebration, but a good time to have the hills for myself and alone seems the best thing for these final days.

The familiarity – walk through the forest again and again but never tire of the depths of needles; plunge my fist in, grasp the sharp golden curls, browning and softening as I dig deeper, further back into the years, dark of the humus beneath, releasing the cool mushroomy smell of woods. Or, this time of year, traceries of cracks and crazings where the pools freeze, thaw and freeze again; night, afternoon, evening. Here opaque, there transparent, shifting from one to another under my weight, the bubbles moving under the glassy plates of ice. Today, my heel breaks right through and the crack rings out across the morning, a big bird sent crashing through the high branches. Maybe the best thing the bleed of resin in the spring after foresting, a weeping wound dripping into a tear and a slowly forming drop. Find it early enough and the sap would stick between my finger and thumb and I would savour the smell all day among the snowfields on top, the north-facing ones remaining through the summer. Find it later and I could pick it off, roll it up into a soft waxen lump with the wee hard outside plasticky bits mixed up in it. I would keep this in my pocket all day, taking it out and breathing in the cool sharpness that would dilate my nostrils and close my eyes.

Leaving the woods and the big boulders beside the path where she would sit with me and listen to the burn gathering power with its rush in the distance. We would look for the distant shapes at the top of the ridge and then train the binoculars on the pair of eagles that we knew played there on the skyline, disappearing behind, rising above. Once, on a clear October afternoon, a shadow, suddenly emblazoned, glided across the dead bracken, sweeping over the gilded rocks, dipping below the crags, lit by the bronze disc dying on the other side of the glen. Earlier that year we had climbed up out of the tumble of boulder and scree up to the right and lay down among the patches of heather in the dried-up peat bogs, where the parched land had cracked and fissured into a lunar dryness. Just as I drifted on the edge of slumber, a light hand touched my arm. I tensed and started up, she with an index finger on her lips and the other hand pointing straight above, skywards, to where the eagles sailed. The same pair nested in the glen for a decade, moving from eyrie to eyrie across their territory of thousands of acres. Then they were gone. Above us they played on the thermals for an hour that day, two silhouettes soaring, circling, becoming one shape for a moment then falling, departing.

Instead of taking the track, head up the narrow defile to gain the rise before the plateau. Today choked with rocks, ice and snow. Glad of the ice axe for balance and leverage, though the terrain too mixed for crampons to be of any use. A memory of the same place two springs ago when, among the saturated moss and slippery rock, the carcass of a deer less than a year old, maybe starved to death after the hardness of a first winter. Crows and insects had half cleaned it and the skull sits in my living room, parchment white and cool to touch. Age betrayed by the unerupted molars in the back of the lower jaw, visible under a fine mesh of bone, a fragile tracery, delicate filigree like something made. Going up through the contours and I can feel the cold sharpen in the breeze from the cloud banks in the north, threatening to stiffen into a wind by midday. Zip up the jacket, grip the ice axe a bit more tightly and feel for the compass in the map pocket, just in case. Further, I can sense things hardening underfoot and think about putting on the crampons.

Scanning the ridge and a line of deer, just the aristocratic heads visible against the skyline, maybe sniffing snow in the air. Look down and suddenly they aren't there. One of the strangest days in the glen, the first time we heard the stags in October in the rutting season. Neither of us expecting it, neither of us recognising it; a low dangerous roar from one side of the glen answered from somewhere else, over and over. Not a noise you'd think could come from a living thing in Scotland. The same day we saw two of them fighting, just visible on the ridge, horns clattering together then apart then into a shove again. Some of the corpes seen in spring would be the defeated from such fights; pushed over the edge of a corrie into freefall, hurtling and tumbling on to crags below with a crash of flesh, antler and bone. The first time I found the aftermath of a gralloching in November, a great coil of blue innards and the grey-white bag of the stomach, full of the semi-digested grass you could see through the pecked holes where the hoodies had been. The most awesome sight was that time we walked over a rise in the land ahead, beyond the ridge the deer were on just a minute ago. The two of us just roaming, lost in the silence that only happens between two people who are close and alone in the high parts. Over the rise and we froze at the suddenness of two hundred deer there in front of us. Downwind, out of scent and hearing, we startled the biggest herd I'd seen in my life. One instant we were walking, lost in thoughts or in no thoughts at all, the next staring at a dream, then a wave rippling over the moor, moving off as one. Drumming of the hooves splashing up sprays of peatwater as you felt the land rolling underneath your feet. Moments later, a space where they had been, fresh with their odour; urine and droppings, the sharp dark scent of wildness. Slowly moving about the place and looking; hoof-marks delicate for such large animals, everywhere the smell of beasts. At the lip of the ridge the deer back again, just necks and heads visible against the blue. Coming out of the ravine to where the plateau opens up and I realise how sheltered the lee side has been and the wind nearly blows me back as I hit the last stage of the climb, exposed to a wind from the east, sweeping for miles across the scoured land. Hood up, gloves on, storm cuffs and velcro fastened. Uneasy when you see on the next range the big reefs of cloud hanging over the tops, closing in above the scree. Wind could bring that over in less than an hour, depending.

Sooner than expected the snowclouds drift across the hills on the other side of the glen, the tops the same height as the one ahead. I can sense the storm coming and now there's no near hills to see. You can tell how high you are, not just because of the ferocity of the wind – that often happened entering the plateau in winter – but it was that sound I hadn't heard for a long time; the harsh, throaty croak, drumming faster and faster til, with a blur of white and bits of grey and black, something you thought was a rock whirrs past your face. The ptarmigan telling me that I'm over two and a half thousand feet up and not far from the tops. Remembering now how bizarre the mountain landscape is in winter, so alien that it helped me to lose an interest in drugs when I was young – some of the things I saw in nature were more powerful than chemicals and I became addicted to the hills, my drug for years. Now, I've been out of the car park for three hours after driving for an hour and a half from the city and in a place weirder than any drug, mostly made so by wind and snow, freezing and thawing. Weather forming an ever-changing sculpture of the summits, the wind-formed snow in ridges and valleys, smoothed into layers or cracked into great slabs, which would sometimes blow loose, smashing and scattering in the wind. Prevailing wind would blow over the snow and it would melt during the day if the sun came through, then halt in strange shapes as the wind freezes it over, making it look more like an Arctic land than Scotland. Even better when the new snow falls powdery and doesn't attach to the layers beneath and drifts like white sand, ghosting across the landscape like it's doing now, a whispering mist in thin veils, rolling like pale smoke, coiling a few feet above ground. Times like these you can kneel or even lie prone in the snow, pointed into the oncoming wind, losing all sense of scale, the furrows and dips starting to look like a great space with a storm blowing across it and you, God-like, gazing down through the clouds at it from a few inches above. This was the strangeness that took me back again and again into the winter mountains, though I never came alone and now I have to.

Still some blue above the flurries but less and less, a strengthening wind lifting everything into a swirl. Soon enough the real snow starting to fall, temperature dropping and dropping. Scenes like this gave memories to look back on but disturbed at the time; best remembered in future as a past event, but the experience unsettling. This time less of an edge to the fear, though; less thought of consequence and less sense of the possibility of loss. Going back in conditions like these would once have been the only way but going on the chosen way now. No word left, nobody hurt. Just me in the landscape, alone on the plateau, ready to take the experience a stage further than ever before and let it run and see where it leads, see how it ends. What's nature like when I cross the boundary and go far beyond where I would have faced away in other times?

I know where I am now even in the white wind. Keep to the fence dividing the two old counties, joining one top across the bealach and on to the next summit, no dropping below three thousand. All that's needed is the compass bearing that I could take even in the swirling white to lead from the fence posts leaning back from the wind, to where the contours start to drop again then to the slightly rising ground across to the summit cairn, a great jumble of massive grey granite boulders heaped like an ancient grave. Easy to be lost in the vast spaces here and some have died, the whole plateau over three thousand feet and nothing much to go on if you lose the cairn from the fence. A man and woman died a year ago in this place, freezing to death in an embrace twenty yards from the cairn, the area I'm pacing right now. The fence posts a good guide to wind direction in winter; a great pennant of ice distorting the shape of the post, droplets freezing and clinging on the lee side, bits of the remaining fence wire broken and twisted with beards of ice hanging off, breaking off, flying away.

After the cairn, tracing a way back to the fence impossible now without a compass. No tracks left from footprints minutes ago; nothing but the white-out. All distance, all scale, gone; no near, no far. A clump of rocks half a metre in front and six inches high now a cliff edge with a two-hundred-foot fall looming out of the whiteness ahead. The white-out howling and all fours the only way now, facing away from the driven blast. Looking down through the swirl and a perfect island surrounded by lagoon, reef and waves, groves of trees everywhere, sand round the edges, seen from miles above. Tranced by a square metre of snow, heather and ice; crawling, laughing and losing it and knowing it could all be thrown away. Vanish into 2000, fade into the storm, dancing points flicker across the static of blinding silver and the soundtrack blasting waves and waves and waves pulsing into a white perfect blur erasing everything

tracery of branches an April evening shades of freshness and light and everything new leaves grass and buds more greens than I ever imagined or dreamed and blossom drifting like pink snow beyond yellow and grey-green of the daffodils and above so many shades of cloud and blue and in between the river glinting and flickering silver-white and grey and the sprays of birdsong liquid and bubbling everywhere with the wee towns on the other side and life going on and night falling gently the lights distant and twinkling a secret code of possibilities

possibilities

too many possibilities to let go now

and years ahead

On Leaving A Volume of Søren Kierkegaard's *Fear and Trembling* in the Back Room of the Campbeltown Bar, Dundee

On Leaving A Volume of Søren Kierkegaard's *Fear and Trembling* in the Back Room of the [illegible] Dancer

Returning ten minutes later, scanning my now occupied seat I feign composure and approach the bar.

'Donald, did anybody hand in a book?'

'Aye.'

He reaches under the counter. I try to avoid the stares of the front room as he looks at the back cover, frowns, looks at the front cover where Søren Kierkegaard glowers back at him.

He stares at me, hands me the book and is about to say something when a voice asserts:

'Crisps? A dear fuckin wey o eatin a tattie.'

A Note on the Author

Bill Duncan was born in St Andrews and spent his childhood in the fishing communities of the East Neuk of Fife, before moving to the outskirts of Dundee. He teaches English in a secondary school and divides his time between Broughty Ferry, Dundee and the Outer Hebrides.

A Note on the Type

The text of this book is set in Linotype Sabon, named after the type founder, Jacques Sabon. It was designed by Jan Tschichold and jointly developed by Linotype, Monotype and Stempel, in response to a need for a typeface to be available in identical form for mechanical hot-metal composition and hand composition using foundry type.

Tschichold based his design for Sabon roman on a fount engraved by Garamond, and Sabon italic on a fount by Granjon. It was first used in 1966 and has proved an enduring modern classic.